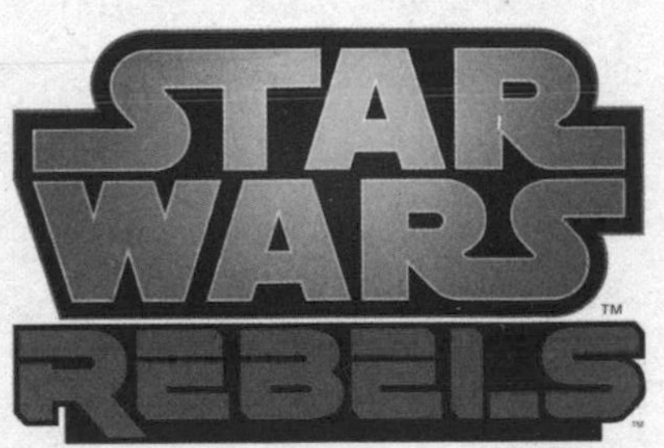
STAR WARS™
REBELS™

ALSO FROM JOE BOOKS

Star Wars: A New Hope Cinestory Comic

Spark of Rebellion: A Star Wars Rebels Cinestory Comic

Path of the Jedi: A Star Wars Rebels Cinestory Comic

Marvel Thor: Dueling with Giants

Marvel Guardians of the Galaxy: Castaways

Marvel Captain America: Sub Rosa

Marvel Sif: Even Dragons Have Their Endings

Marvel Warriors Three: Godhood's End

Marvel Guardians of the Galaxy: Space Riot

Marvel Iron Man: Mutually Assured Destruction

Marvel Spider-Man: Enemies Closer

Marvel Avengers: The Serpent Society

Marvel Captain America: The Never-Ending Battle

Marvel Thor: Crusade of the Forgotten

STAR WARS™ REBELS™

MAUL

CINESTORY COMIC

JOE BOOKS LTD

Published simultaneously in the United States and Canada by
Joe Books Ltd, 489 College Street, Suite 203, Toronto, ON M6G 1A5.

www.joebooks.com

First Joe Books edition: February 2018

Print ISBN: 978-1-77275-635-7
ebook ISBN: 978-1-77275-865-8

Library and Archives Canada Cataloguing in Publication information is available upon request.

Printed and bound in Canada
1 3 5 7 9 10 8 6 4 2

CONTENTS

TWILIGHT OF THE APPRENTICE

THE PHANTOM, HYPERSPACE.

ONCE WE DROP OUT OF HYPERSPACE, WE'LL BE GOING DARK.

ARE YOU SURE ABOUT THIS?
YES.

AHSOKA, YOU DON'T HAVE TO GO TO MALACHOR ALONE. I COULD BE THERE IN TWO ROTATIONS.

I'M NOT ALONE, REX.

YOU KNOW, I COULD HAVE ORDERED YOU TO TAKE ME ALONG.

YOU DON'T EXACTLY OUTRANK ME ANYMORE.
IN MY BOOK, EXPERIENCE OUTRANKS EVERYTHING.

HMM, THEN I DEFINITELY OUTRANK YOU.

MAY THE FORCE BE WITH YOU.

WHY IS REX SO WORRIED? WHAT DOES HE KNOW THAT I DON'T?

MALACHOR HAS ALWAYS BEEN OFF LIMITS TO JEDI.

WHY?

SIGH
OLD LEGENDS-- STORIES TOLD TO US AS YOUNGLINGS IN THE TEMPLE.

THERE'S ALWAYS A BIT OF *TRUTH* IN LEGENDS.

IF MALACHOR IS OFF LIMITS, WHY WOULD MASTER YODA SEND US HERE?

MALACHOR.

I DON'T KNOW, BUT I TRUST MASTER YODA. THERE'S SOMETHING HERE FOR US.

YEAH, SOMETHING TO HELP US STOP THE INQUISITORS.

KNOWLEDGE.

WUP BUP WUP BUH
BUH BUH BUP

A SHIP?
WHAT TYPE?
WHUU BUP BUP

-SIGH- HE CAN'T TELL.

TRACK IT. LET'S SEE WHO ELSE IS INTERESTED IN THIS PLACE.

LOOK UP AHEAD. WHAT IS THAT?

I DON'T KNOW, BUT THE SHIP WE'RE TRACKING WENT THERE. I'M GONNA SET HER DOWN.

I DON'T SEE ANY SHIP.

IT'S GOTTA BE AROUND HERE SOMEWHERE.

CHOPPER, TRY TO GET A FIX ON ITS LOCATION.

WUP BUH

WHAT ARE THESE THINGS?

THIS WRITING... IT'S IN THE *OLD TONGUE.*

CAN YOU READ IT?

SIGH I CAN TRY. IT'S A VERY OLD FORM... I CAN ONLY MAKE OUT A FEW WORDS.

TAKA... ZEECH MA TOKA... DUUWAG...

NO! EZRA, DON'T!

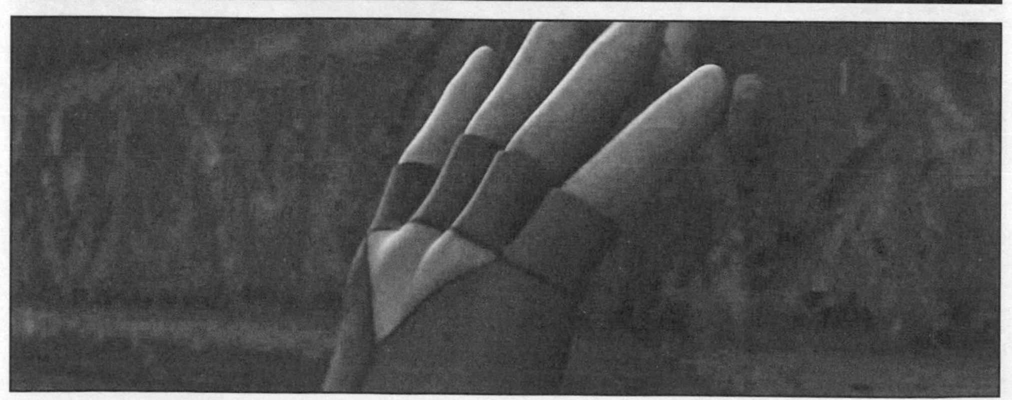

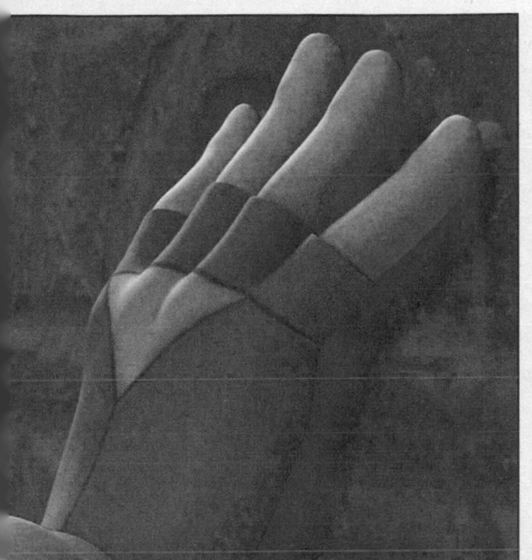

WHOA!
AAH!
CRACK
AAAHH!

WW--
AAAAHHHHH!

OOF!
UNGH!

AARGH!

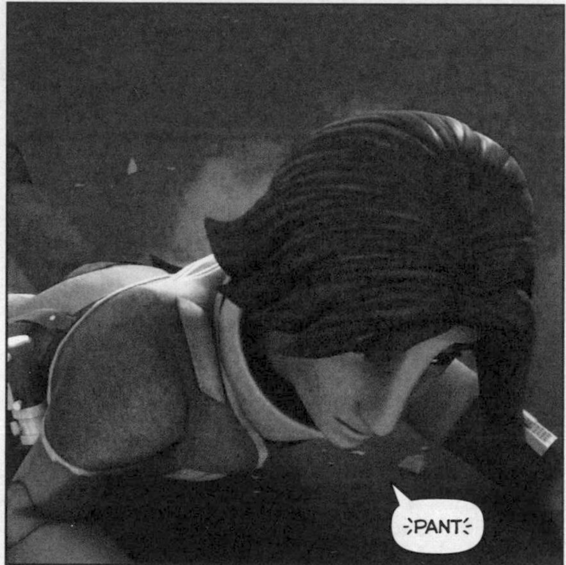
PANT

PANT WHAT IS *THAT?*

A SITH TEMPLE.

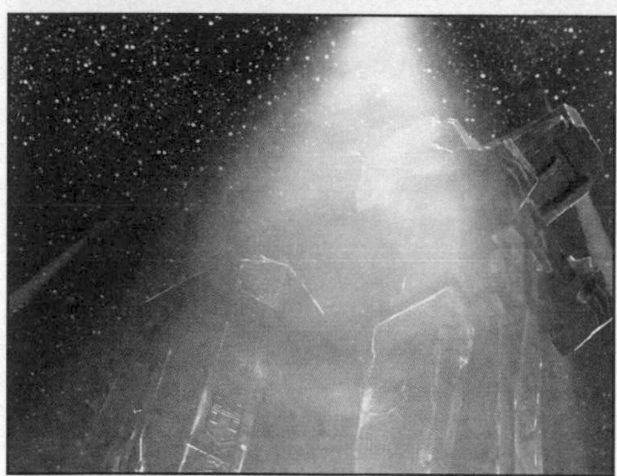

WHU BUP BUP WHUP

OH, WE MIGHT FALL THROUGH THE SURFACE? THANKS FOR THE WARNING, CHOP.

ANY FIX ON THAT SHIP YET?

WHUP BUH BUH

HE'S PICKED UP THE TRAIL-- THIS WAY.

I BET WHATEVER WE'RE LOOKING FOR IS INSIDE THAT TEMPLE.

SEEMS LIKELY. JUST REMEMBER, IF THERE'S A SHIP, WE'RE NOT ALONE DOWN HERE.

AHSOKA, YOU SAID WE'RE HERE TO FIND KNOWLEDGE. WHAT *KIND* OF KNOWLEDGE?

THE *FORBIDDEN* KIND. TO DEFEAT YOUR ENEMY, YOU HAVE TO *UNDERSTAND* THEM.

NO BETTER PLACE TO LEARN ABOUT THE SITH, I GUESS.

THE GROUND LOOKS SCORCHED. *WHOA*, KANAN! LOOK, A *LIGHTSABER!*

AND ANOTHER.

TSSSHEW

TSSSHEW

FZZZZ

THIS WAS A *BATTLEFIELD.*

WHAT HAPPENED HERE?

IT LOOKS LIKE AT ONE TIME, THOUSANDS OF YEARS AGO, JEDI KNIGHTS ATTACKED THE TEMPLE.

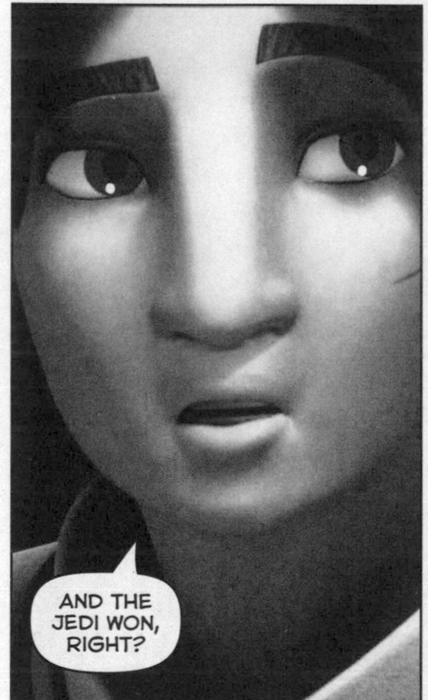
AND THE JEDI WON, RIGHT?

FROM WHAT I CAN TELL, *NOBODY* WON.

I HATE TO BREAK UP THIS HISTORY LESSON, BUT WE SHOULD KEEP MOVING.

WELL, IF YOU ASK ME, THIS WHOLE PLANET IS A RIDDLE.

SO IF IT'S A RIDDLE, WHAT'S THE *QUESTION?*

WHY IS KANAN SUCH A--

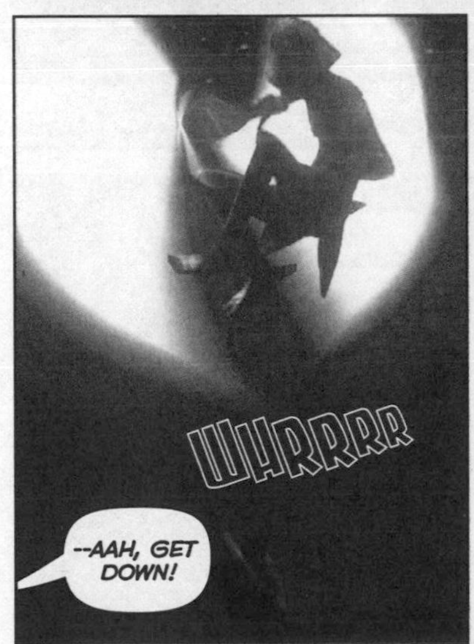
WHRRRR
--AAH, GET DOWN!

CRKTCHAK

THREE JEDI?

AN INQUISITOR!

TAKE COVER!

FASHOOM

TCHAAAACK

KANAN!

EZRA!

EZRA, CAN YOU HEAR ME?

ARGH... I'M OKAY.

HE'S GETTING AWAY! LET'S GO!

DON'T WORRY ABOUT ME, I'LL CATCH UP!

WHRRR

SIGH SURE, I'LL CATCH UP... SOON AS I FIGURE OUT WHERE I AM.

I KNOW WHERE YOU ARE. YOU'RE WITH *ME.* *HEH.*

PLEASE PUT YOUR WEAPON AWAY. I-I MEAN YOU NO HARM.

STAY BACK! I'M WARNING YOU, OLD MAN.

FORGIVE ME, IT-IT'S JUST, I'VE BEEN ALONE SO LONG. I-IT'S BEEN YEARS SINCE I'VE SPOKEN TO ANYONE.

YOU LIVE HERE ALONE? IN THE DARK?

NOT BY CHOICE. MY SHIP CRASHED. I'M TRAPPED, MAROONED. I'VE HAD TO SCROUNGE AND SCRAPE TO SURVIVE.

LOOK, I'M SORRY. OKAY? I WISH I COULD HELP YOU, BUT I HAVE TO GET BACK TO MY FRIENDS.

WELL, PERHAPS I COULD HELP YOU.

I DOUBT THAT.

WHY ARE YOU HERE?

I'M NOT GONNA TELL YOU THAT.

YOU CAME FOR THE SAME REASON I DID, YEARS AGO. YOU SEEK KNOWLEDGE.

IT'S IN THE TEMPLE, ISN'T IT?

AND I KNOW THE SECRET WAY TO GET INSIDE, BUT-BUT I'M TOO OLD. I-I-I NEED HELP TO OPEN THE DOOR.

WHAT'S INSIDE?

HELP ME AND FIND OUT.

SHOW ME THIS DOORWAY.

PLEASE, THIS WAY.

YOU FIRST.

DO YOU NOT *TRUST* ME?

I DON'T *KNOW* YOU.

W-WELL, THEN LET'S CHANGE THAT. CALL ME... *"OLD MASTER."*

AND YOU?

CALL ME "JABBA."

HMM. COME THEN... JABBA.

ZZZZ

I'VE NEVER HAD AN INQUISITOR RUN FROM *ME* BEFORE.

MAYBE IT'S BECAUSE HE'S OUTNUMBERED.

HE DID SEEM SURPRISED. I DON'T THINK HE WAS LOOKING FOR US.

THEN WHO IS HE TRACKING?

HMM...
WHUP WHUP WHUP
BUH BUP

YOU FOUND THE SHIP? *WHERE?*

WHUH WHUP WHUP WHUP

NO, NO. FORGET IT, NO TIME! GET OVER THERE AND FIND THAT SHIP.
DO *NOT* LET HIM TAKE OFF! WE'LL FOLLOW YOUR SIGNAL.

WHUUUH BUP BUP BUP
NO, DISOBEYING ***ME*** IS GONNA BE DANGEROUS. ***NOW GET GOING!***

WHUH WHUP BUP BUP

FWOOM

FWOOSH

HOW MUCH FARTHER?

YOU WORRY ABOUT YOUR FRIENDS?
THEY NEED MY HELP.

YES...SIGH...AND WITH GOOD REASON. THE INQUISITOR IS POWERFUL.

WAIT...YOU KNOW ABOUT THE INQUISITOR?

HE IS MY ENEMY. *ALL* INQUISITORS AND THEIR MASTERS ARE MY ENEMIES.

WERE YOU A *JEDI?*

NO. NO, NO. BUT I WAS ONCE A *FORCE-WIELDER*, LONG AGO. LONG, LONG AGO.

THEN YOU'RE A *SITH?*

THE SITH...THE SITH TOOK *EVERYTHING* FROM ME. RIPPED ME FROM MY MOTHER'S ARMS, MURDERED MY BROTHER, USED ME AS A WEAPON, AND THEN CAST ME ASIDE.
ABANDONED ME. ONCE, I HAD POWER... NOW I HAVE NOTHING. *NOTHING.*
I KNOW HOW YOU FEEL.

THE EMPIRE, IT TOOK AWAY MY HOME, AND MY MOTHER, AND MY FATHER.

AND YOU WANT REVENGE.

I WANT *JUSTICE!*

YES, *YES!* AND YOU SHALL HAVE IT...FOR I HAVE DISCOVERED THE *KEY.*

THE KEY TO WHAT?

THE KEY TO *DESTROYING* THE SITH.

THAT IS THE KNOWLEDGE INSIDE THE TEMPLE?

YES, THAT TEMPLE HOLDS SECRETS OF THE SITH, SECRETS THAT HAVE BEEN BURIED WITH THE DEAD FOR THOUSANDS OF YEARS.

AND YOU'LL SHARE THIS KNOWLEDGE WITH ME?
YES. YES, OF COURSE.

WHUP BUH BUH
FWOOSH

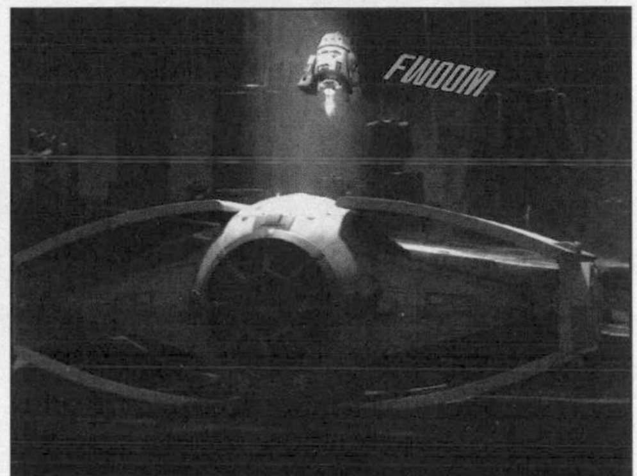
FWOOM

WHUP BUP WHUP BUP

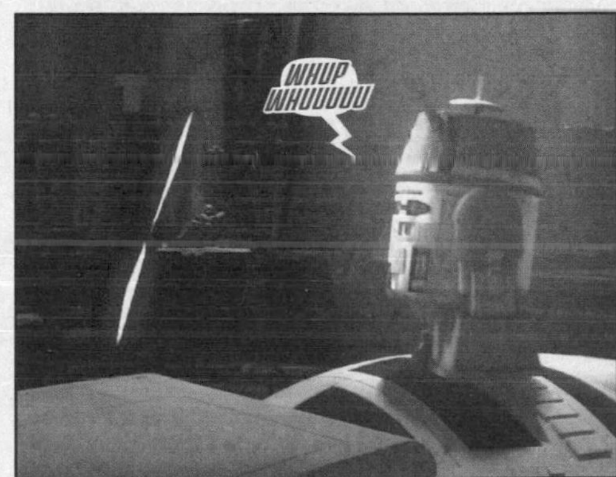
WHUP WHUUUUU

WHRRR
WHUP

WHUP BUP WHUP WHUP WHUP

FILTHY DROID.

WHUP BUH

WHUP WHUP BUH BUH BUH

KSHOOM
KSHOOM

KSHOOOM

KSHOOM

RNGH.
THUD

WUPWUPWUP

NGH.

UGH--

CHOPPER, SOMETIMES YOU DO IT RIGHT.

WHUWHU BUP BUP BUP!

WHOA.

A PLACE OF *WORSHIP* FOR SOME. TO OTHERS, AN ENGINE OF *DESTRUCTION.*

BUT AT ITS HEART, OUR *PRIZE.*

HOW DO WE GET IN?

TWO MUST LIFT THESE STONES. NO MORE, NO LESS. *THAT* IS THE WAY OF THE SITH.

YOU SEEM TO KNOW AN AWFUL LOT ABOUT THEM.

TO DEFEAT YOUR ENEMY, YOU MUST KNOW YOUR ENEMY. EVEN PRACTICE THEIR BELIEFS.

YEAH... MY MASTER WOULDN'T APPROVE OF THAT LAST PART.

THEN HE IS DOOMED TO FAIL.
SIGH
NOW, YOUNG JEDI, HELP ME.

UNGH.
I CAN'T. IT'S TOO HEAVY.

YOUR ANGER IS A WELLSPRING. YOU MUST *USE* IT.

BUT...A JEDI IS *NEVER* SUPPOSED TO ACT OUT OF EMOTION.

YOUR PASSIONS GIVE YOU STRENGTH. AND THROUGH *STRENGTH,* YOU GAIN *POWER.* YOU HAVE SEEN IT. YOU *FEEL* IT. YOU *MUST* BREAK YOUR CHAINS.

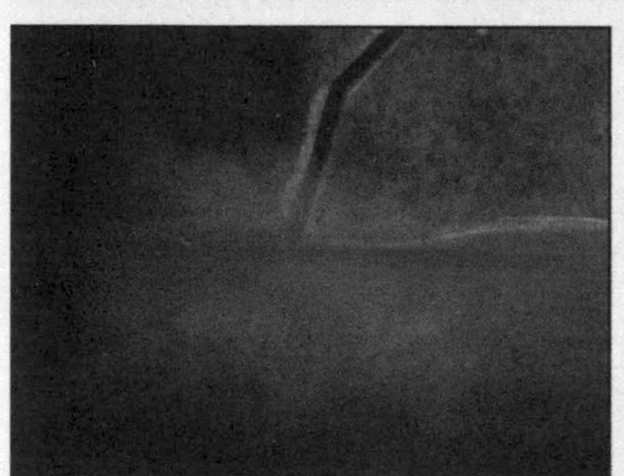

YES...USE YOUR POWER.

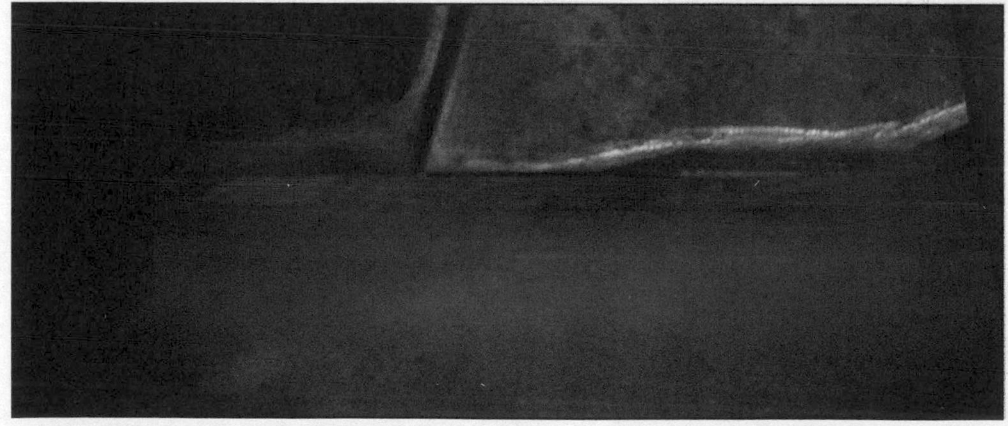

ARGH...
RUMBLE

A DEAD END!

FOCUS!

WHAT DO WE DO?

RRGH... RELEASE THE ONE BEHIND YOU.

THUD

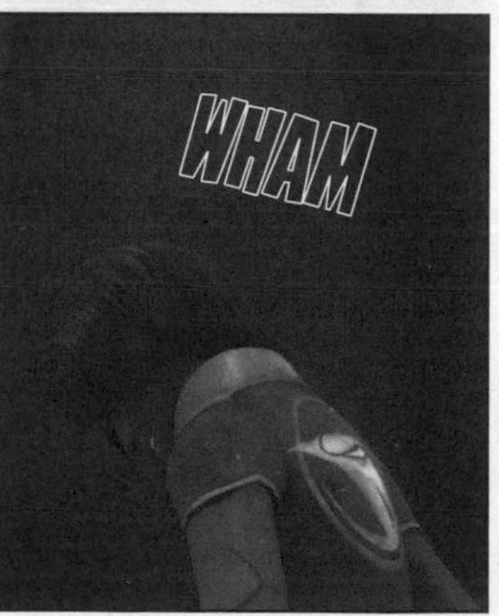
WHAM

ARGH. HOW MANY OF THESE THINGS ARE THERE?

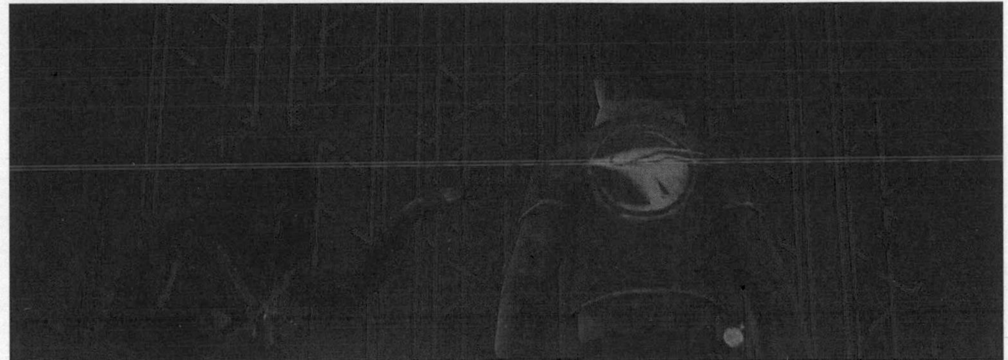

NN... RRGH!

UGH.
AARG.

SLAM

COUGH, COUGH
SIGH UNLESS YOU TAKE RISKS, DO WHAT MUST BE DONE, THERE WILL ALWAYS BE LIMITS TO YOUR ABILITIES. SEIZE THE KNOWLEDGE.

SEIZE THE POWER. DO NOT BECOME LIKE ME, JABBA.

MY NAME'S EZRA. MY REAL NAME.

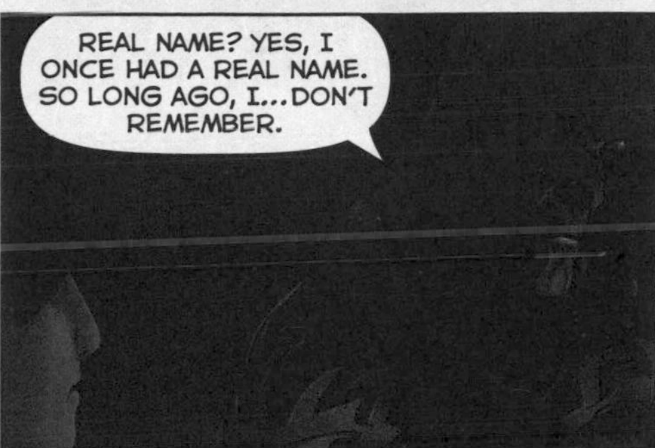
REAL NAME? YES, I ONCE HAD A REAL NAME. SO LONG AGO, I...DON'T REMEMBER.

NOW...NOW I AM CALLED... *MAUL.*

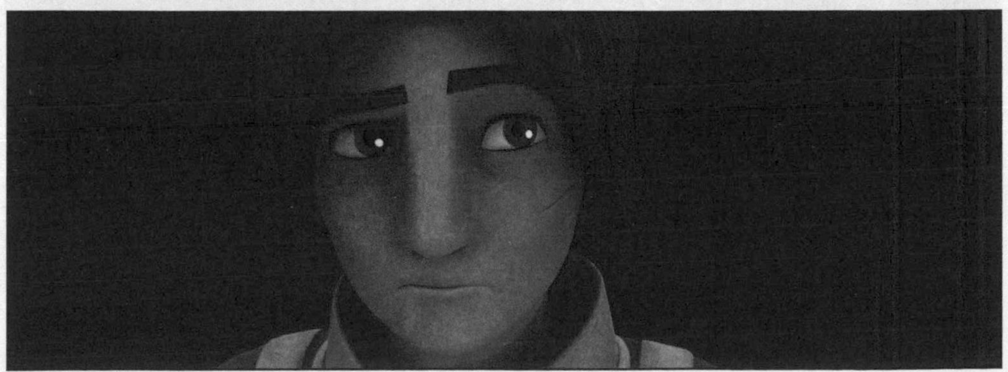

YOU'RE THE FOURTH INQUISITOR WE'VE SEEN. HOW MANY ARE THERE?

MORE THAN ENOUGH FOR THE TWO OF YOU.

HEH. NOTHING CAN SAVE YOU.

WHY ARE YOU ON MALACHOR?

HUNTING.

BUT YOU WERE NOT EXPECTING US WHO ARE YOU AFTER?

HA-HA-HA. A SHADOW.

BEHOLD... THE KEY.

IT'S A *HOLOCRON.*

YOU KNOW OF THEM?

YEAH. MY MASTER HAS ONE, BUT...IT'S DIFFERENT.

BECAUSE THIS IS A *SITH* HOLOCRON, ONE THAT HOLDS ALL THEIR SECRETS.

WELL, HOW DO WE GET TO IT?

IT IS A *TEST.* ONLY SOMEONE WITH THE COURAGE TO RISK *OBLIVION* IS WORTHY TO CLAIM IT.

THROW ME.

YEAH, THROW ME. I'LL JUMP, AND THEN YOU USE THE FORCE TO THROW ME. MY MASTER AND I DO IT ALL THE TIME.
WELL... A FEW TIMES ANYWAY.

LOOK, WE CAN *DO* THIS.

OOF
AAAH! WHOAAAH! AAAAHHH!

UNGH
SIGH
THUNK

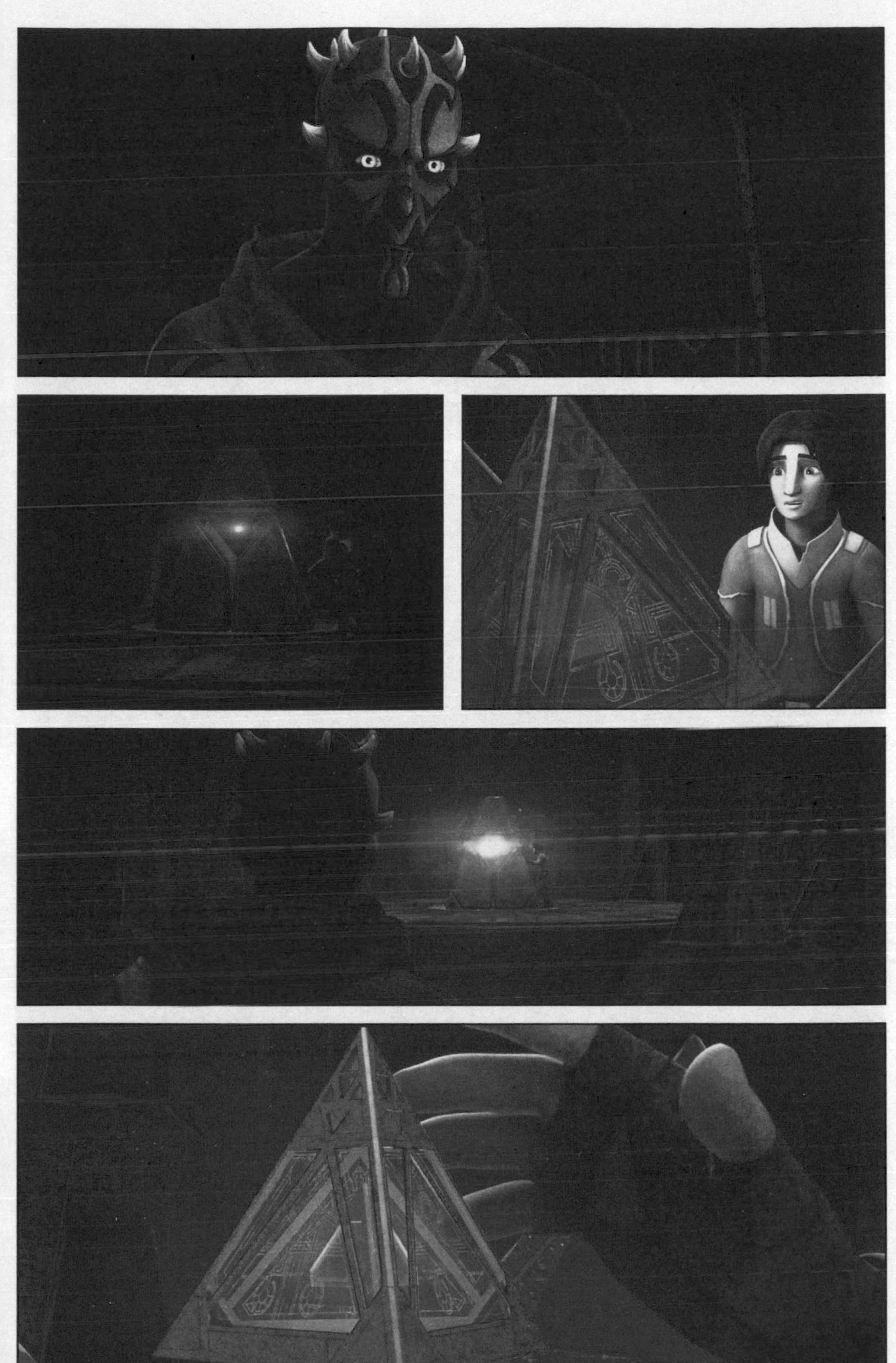

RUMBLE

BEEP

WE NEED TO FIND EZRA.

GET BACK TO THE *PHANTOM* AND GET READY TO LEAVE.

WHUP WHUP WHUP

COME ON, LET'S TAKE A WALK.

CRRTZZZZ

JUMP!

I WON'T MAKE IT!

VRZZZZZ

EZRA!

I CAN'T!

WHY DO I KNOW EZRA'S INVOLVED IN THIS SOMEHOW?

TRUST ME!

AH--

AAAHHHHHHHHH!

HRRGH.

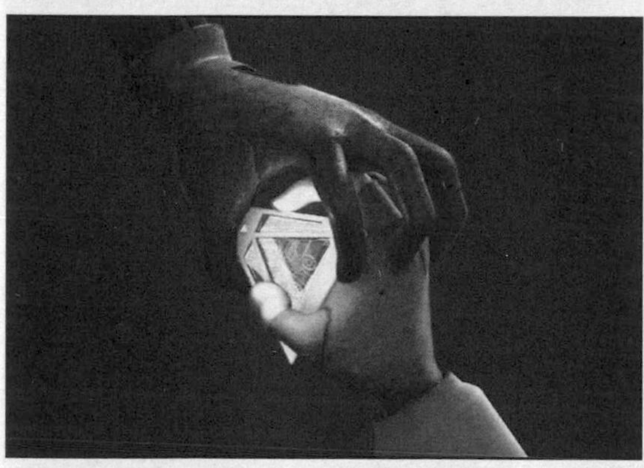

NNGH.

THERE WAS NOTHING TO FEAR. YOU WERE WISE TO TRUST ME.

HE'S INSIDE, I KNOW IT. BUT THERE'S *NO WAY* HE LIFTED THAT DOOR.

NOT WITHOUT HELP.

HEH-HEH-HEH.
WHAT'S SO FUNNY?

WHAT IS IT CHOPPER?
WHUH WHUP BUH BUP

BUH BUH BUP BUH
WHAT DO YOU MEAN *WE'VE GOT COMPANY?*

HA-HA-HA-HA-HA.
HEY, WHAT ARE YOU LAUGHING AT?

WHRRR

TSSSHEW
TSSSHEW

WHHRRRRR

CRKTCHAK

AN EXCELLENT DAY'S HUNT.

HOW DO YOU OPEN THIS?

ONE MUST BE A SITH. OR *THINK* LIKE ONE. BUT IT HAS, *HMM, OTHER USES.*
GIVE IT TO ME, I WILL SHOW YOU.

SITH HOLOCRONS ARE *KEYS.*

THEY CAN OPEN MANY DOORS.

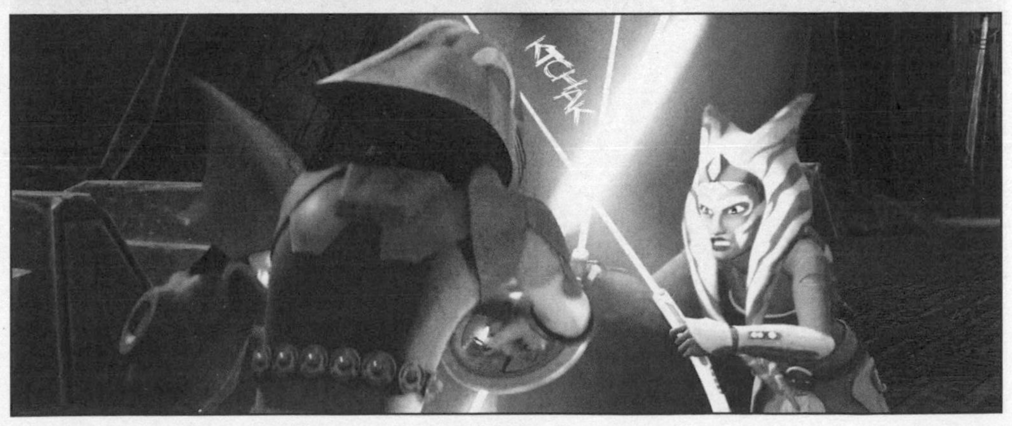
KTCHAK

EZRA!

KANAN, AHSOKA! I BROUGHT HELP.

MAUL.

THE SHADOW.

WHAT FUN.
HEH-HEH. *WHAT FUN!* HA-HA-HA-HA-HA!

SO, THE RUMORS ARE TRUE. DARTH MAUL LIVES.

FORMERLY DARTH, NOW JUST *MAUL.*

EZRA, STEP AWAY FROM HIM!

KANAN, I SWEAR HE'S ON OUR SIDE!

PERHAPS MY ACTIONS WILL SPEAK LOUDER THAN WORDS.

TSSSHEW

TKZZZ

WHAT ARE WE WAITING FOR?

KRTZZ
WHY WOULD YOU COME HERE?
HE KNOWS OF THE ARTIFACT!

ZRTZZ

THE HOLOCRON--
DO YOU HAVE IT?
SZZ

YOU WILL
FIND OUT SOON
ENOUGH.

KTCHAK
FALL
BACK!

WHRRRR

MAUL, WHAT GAME ARE YOU PLAYING?

THE END GAME, LADY TANO. THE END GAME.

I AM THE ENEMY OF YOUR ENEMY NOW, AND I HAVE MY OWN REASONS FOR WANTING THE EMPIRE TO FALL.

BUT WE HAVE LITTLE TIME. THE ONE THEY CALL *VADER* WILL BE HERE SOON.

HOW DO YOU KNOW THIS?

HIS DOGS WILL TELL HIM WHERE WE ARE. TWO JEDI AND A...*PART TIMER.*

OH, HE WILL COME. HE WILL NOT BE ABLE TO RESIST US.

OKAY, HOLD ON, THERE IS NO "US." DEALING WITH INQUISITORS IS ONE THING, *VADER* IS ANOTHER.
AND I'M NOT CONVINCED WE'RE ALL ON THE SAME SIDE ANYWAY.

KANAN, WE SHOULD TRUST HIM.

LOOK--HE AND I TOOK THIS FROM THE TEMPLE *TOGETHER.*

THIS IS WHY WE CAME HERE, RIGHT? TO FIND OUT ABOUT THE SITH. TO FIND A WAY TO *BEAT THEM.*

AHSOKA, YOU SAID WE CAME HERE FOR KNOWLEDGE.

EZRA, THERE IS NO WAY A JEDI CAN UNLOCK THAT HOLOCRON.

BUT YOU MAY UNLOCK THE *TEMPLE ITSELF.*

HOW? TELL ME HOW.

AT THE TOP OF THE TEMPLE IS A CHAMBER.

CONNECT THE HOLOCRON TO THE OBELISK WITHIN AND YOU CAN UNLOCK THE ANCIENT KNOWLEDGE OF THE SITH.

WHY ARE YOU WORKING SO HARD TO KEEP US HERE?

I CANNOT DEFEAT VADER ALONE.

I SAY WE STAY WITH HIM.

YEAH? WELL, I SAY WE *GO*, SO THAT SETTLES IT.

ARE YOU SUCH **COWARDS** THAT YOU WOULD RUN FROM THIS CHANCE TO DEFEAT YOUR ENEMIES? WHO SLAUGHTER YOUR FRIENDS?

KANAN?

SIGH

CHOPPER, WE'RE STAYING FOR A WHILE.
WHUH BUH BUP

YEAH, I *KNOW* IT'S A BAD IDEA. JUST SCAN FOR INCOMING SHIPS, AND KEEP THE *PHANTOM* OUT OF SIGHT.
WHUH BUH BUH BUH

OH, HOW EXCITING--WE'RE ALL ON THE SAME SIDE.

JUST SHOW US HOW TO GET TO THE TOP, AND HURRY.
THIS WAY.

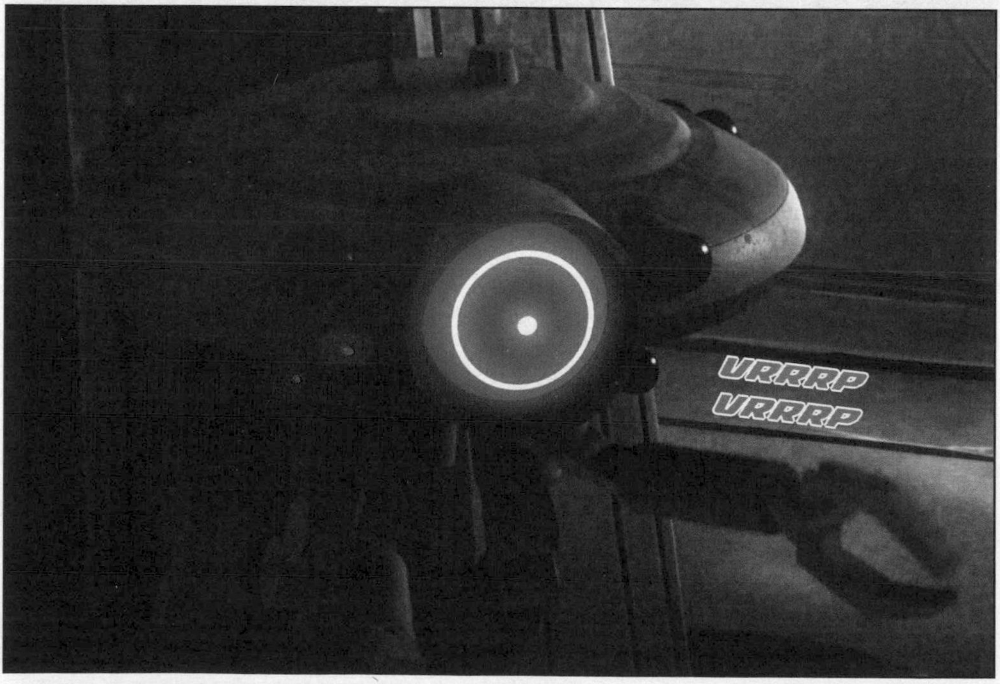

VRRRP
VRRRP

HE AND I TOOK THIS FROM THE TEMPLE TOGETHER. AND THIS IS WHY WE CAME HERE, RIGHT? TO FIND OUT ABOUT THE SITH.

THE BOY HAS THE HOLOCRON.

WE CANNOT ALLOW HIM TO USE IT.

I WILL RECLAIM IT.
TSSSHEW

WAIT! LET HIM THIN THEM OUT, THEN *WE* WILL RETRIEVE LORD VADER'S PRIZE.

NOW WHAT?

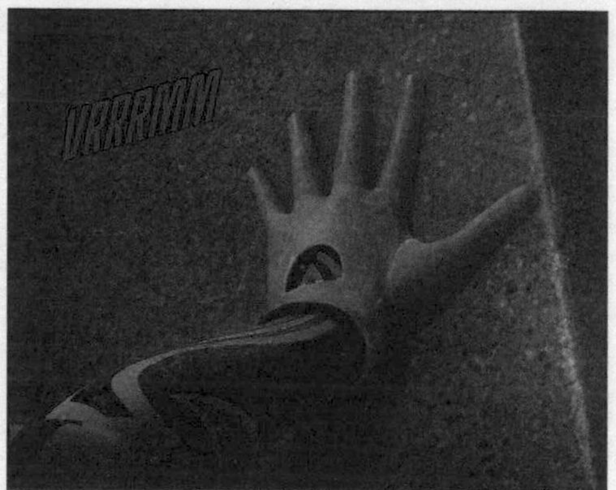
VRRRMM

RRRRRRRR

WOW!

ONLY TWO. NO MORE, NO LESS.

YEAH? WELL, THESE TWO COME AS A SET.

YOU OKAY RIDING WITH GRANDPA?

I'LL BE FINE.

FWWMMMMM

EZRA, LISTEN TO ME, HE'S *USING* YOU.

ARE YOU *EVER* GONNA TRUST ME TO THINK FOR MYSELF? TO FOLLOW MY INSTINCTS?

I *DO* TRUST YOU.

MAUL SEES WHAT I COULD BE. *YOU DON'T.*

HE'LL SAY *ANYTHING* TO GET WHAT HE WANTS.

LOOK OUT!

WHRRR

UGH.
THUD

TSSSHEW

KTCHAK

FWACK

WHOA!

GIVE ME THE HOLOCRON.

WHRRRRRRRR

EZRA!

TKSZZ

WHRRR

WHRRRRRR

LOOKS LIKE THEY'VE FIGURED OUT YOUR PLAN.

THEN WE SHALL ALTER IT. I RECOMMEND THAT WE SPLIT UP AND SCALE THE PYRAMID FROM TWO SIDES. THEY WILL ALSO HAVE TO DIVIDE THEIR FORCES.

AND LET ME GUESS, EZRA GOES WITH *YOU?* NO THANKS.

IT IS THE LOGICAL CHOICE.

I SAY WE SPLIT UP. ***TRUST ME.***

SIGH

EXCELLENT,
EXCELLENT.

YOU WILL FIND ANOTHER LIFT ON THE FAR SIDE, WE WILL MEET AGAIN ON THE NEXT TERRACE.
FWWMMMMM

HE'LL BE FINE.
YEAH? HOW DO YOU KNOW THAT?

BECAUSE... YOU TAUGHT HIM.

THE DARK SIDE FIGHTS WITHOUT MERCY, WITHOUT REMORSE. IF YOU WANT TO BE VICTORIOUS, YOU NEED TO FIND THE SAME STRENGTH INSIDE *YOU.*

KANAN ALWAYS SAID FIGHTING IS A *LAST* RESORT, NOT A FIRST.

EZRA, YOU WERE GIVEN YOUR GIFT FOR ONE REASON--TO USE IT. CAN I COUNT ON YOU?

VRRRRP
VRRRRP

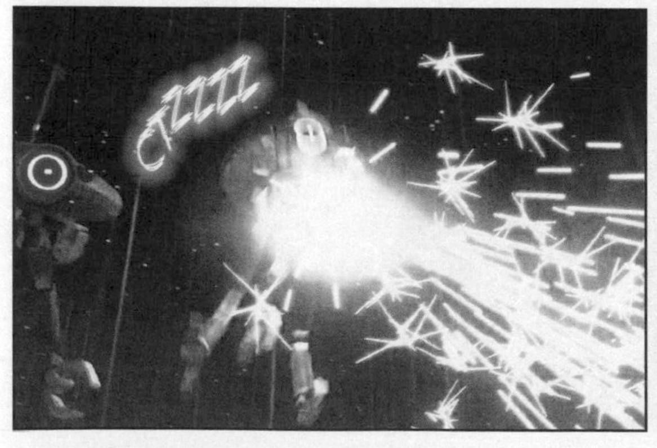
CZZZZ

HA-
HA-HA-HA-
HAH!
TSSSHEW

AAAH!

THAT DOESN'T SOUND GOOD.

LOOK OUT!

TZZNG
TZZNG

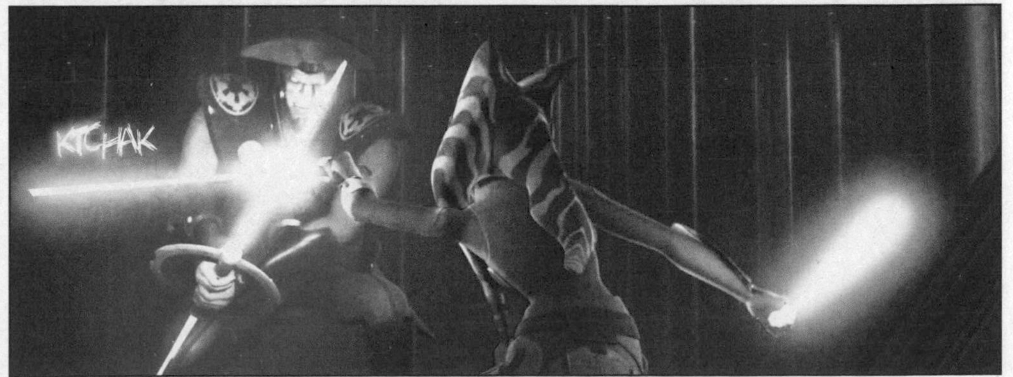
KTCHAK

THAT'S IT, YOUNG ONE. USE YOUR ANGER, USE YOUR PAIN, LET IT FILL YOU...FUEL YOU.

FTZZ

FWOOSH

NO!
NO!

STRIKE HER DOWN!

YOU WANT TO END THIS? FINISH HER!

I CAN'T!

AUGH.
HRRAGH!

VRTZZ
AAHHH!

THE NEXT TIME YOU HESITATE LIKE THAT, IT MAY COST YOU YOUR LIFE... OR THE LIVES OF YOUR FRIENDS.

AGH!
WE MUST HURRY. I FEAR OUR COMPANIONS ARE IN DANGER.

CRKTCHAK

WHAT IS IT?
NOTHING.

WE MUST NOT DELAY. I WILL HANDLE THIS. YOU TAKE THE HOLOCRON.
PLACE IT IN THE OBELISK, ACTIVATE THE TEMPLE, GAIN THE KNOWLEDGE YOU SEEK.

I'LL MEET YOU AT THE TOP.

SZZZ

KTZZ ZT-KRAK

CLANK

ZRRT
AAUGH!

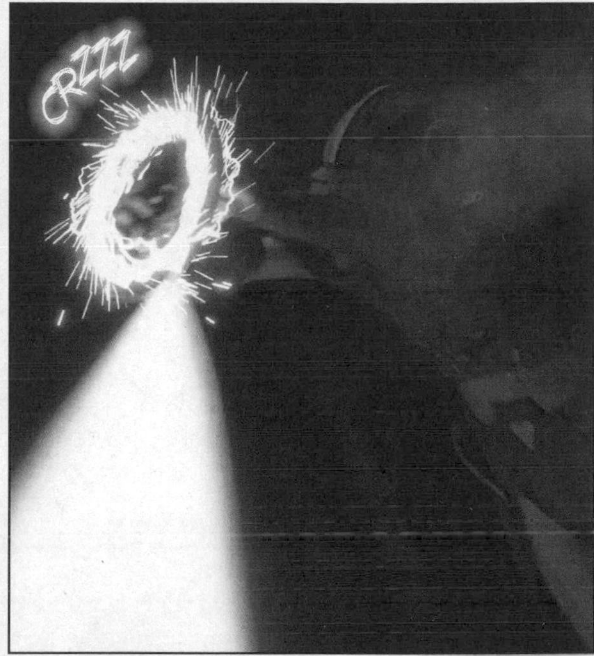
CRZZZ
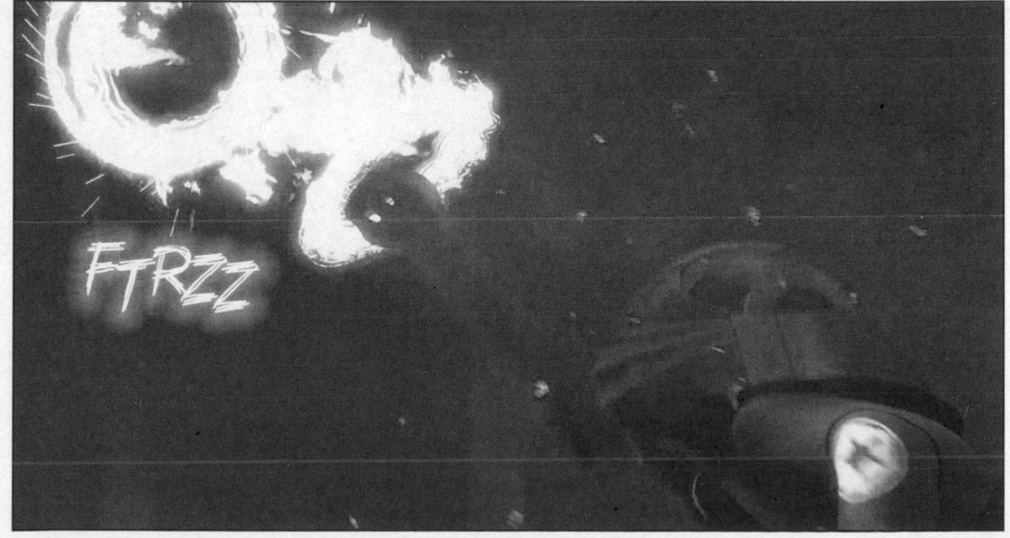
FTRZZ

AAAAHHHHHH!

WHERE'S EZRA?

YOU MEAN...MY APPRENTICE?

FWUWUWM

NRRGH.

KANAN!

MY APPRENTICE IS ACTIVATING THE TEMPLE, OR MORE PRECISELY, THIS *BATTLE STATION*...

...WHICH I SHALL USE TO EXACT MY REVENGE ON *ALL MY ENEMIES!*

CRZZZ

THOOM
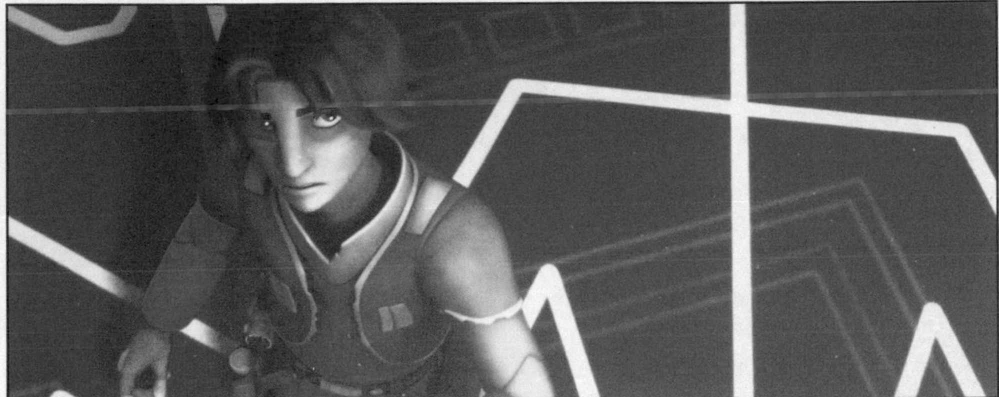
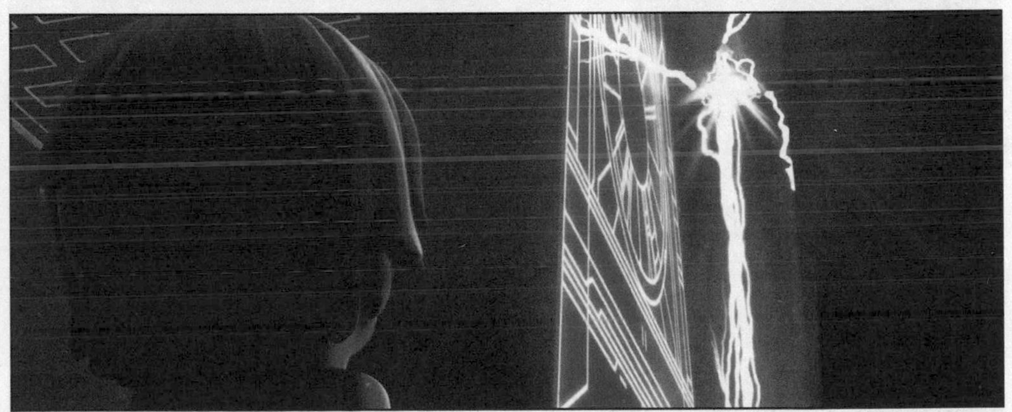

WHO COMES FORTH?

INDEED, EZRA BRIDGER. AND DO YOU KNOW WHAT KNOWLEDGE IS?

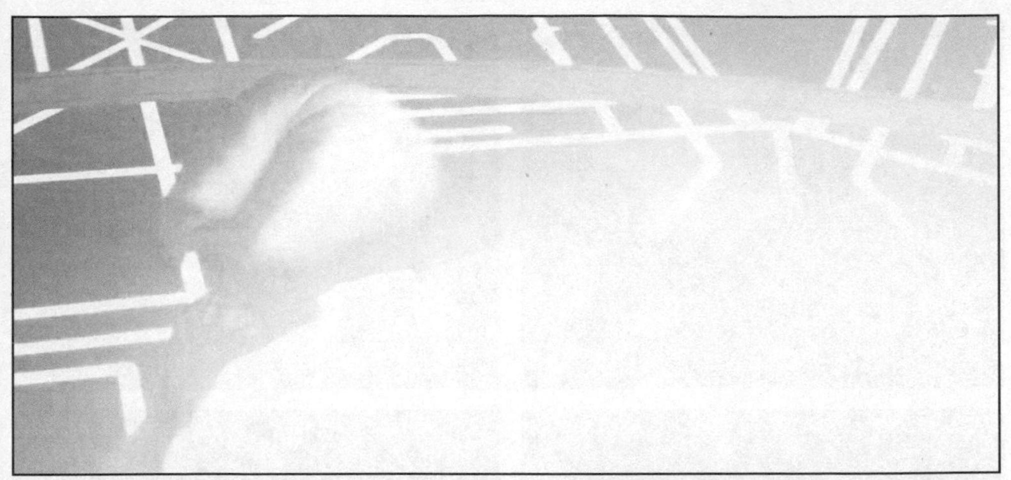

THOOOOM

CRZZZZRT

CRKTCHAK

THE POWER WILL BE *MINE! EZRA* WILL BE *MINE,* AND THERE IS *NOTHING* YOU CAN DO TO STOP ME.

ZTKRAK

RUNNING AWAY *AGAIN*, LADY TANO?

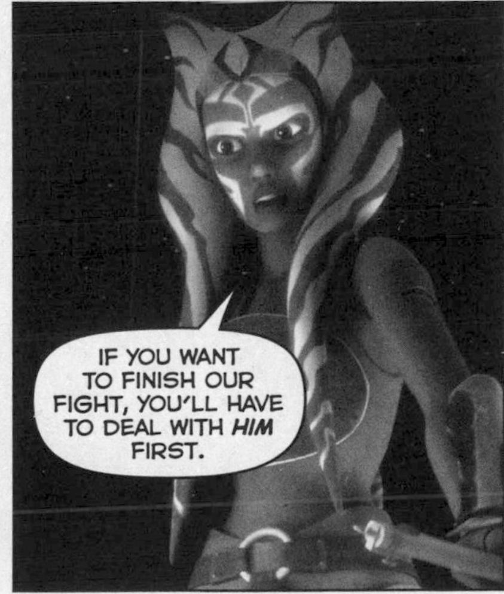
IF YOU WANT TO FINISH OUR FIGHT, YOU'LL HAVE TO DEAL WITH *HIM* FIRST.

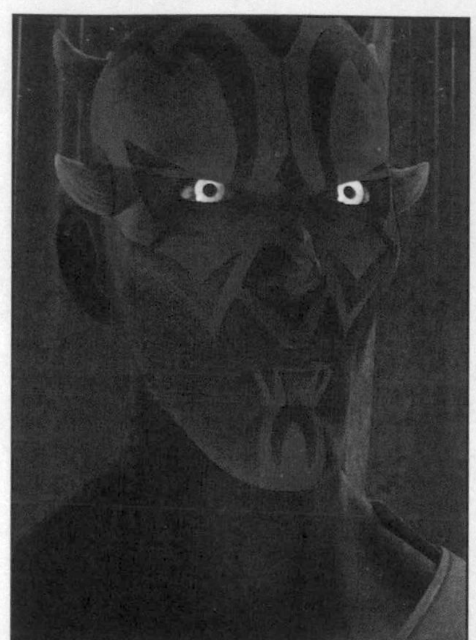

GO GET EZRA!

I WILL MAKE THIS QUICK.
SZZZ

YOU HAD YOUR CHANCE.
TSSSHEW

TKZZZ

KTZZZPKRAK

GASP

AAAARRRGHHH!

SIGH
BUH BUBUP
BUH BUBUP

CHOPPER, AM I GLAD TO HEAR YOU! WE NEED A PICKUP.
BUH BUHBUH BUP

A TIE FIGHTER? ARE YOU SURE?

I HAVE BEEN WAITING.
WHAT'S HAPPENING?

THE POWER TO DESTROY LIFE IS AT YOUR COMMAND.

WHAT? NO! NO, NO! THAT'S NOT WHAT I WANTED!
THEN PERHAPS THE OTHER WHO APPROACHES WILL CLAIM IT INSTEAD.

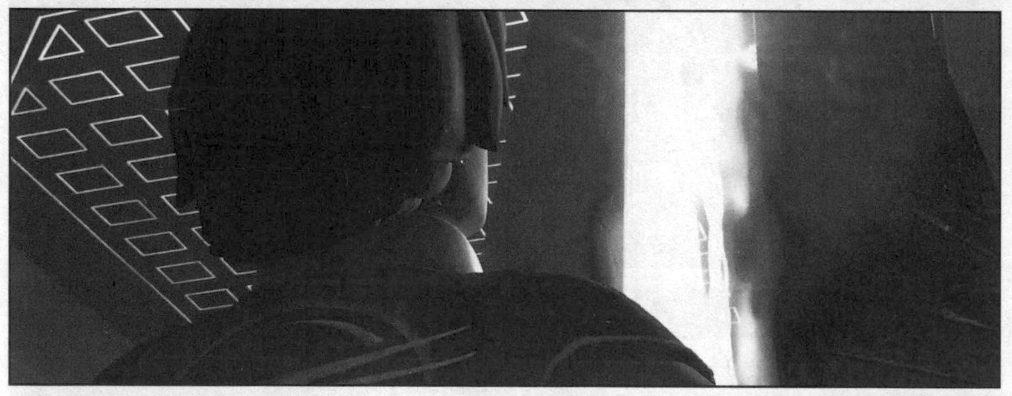

MAUL.

KANAN, AHSOKA, MAUL TRICKED US! THIS TEMPLE'S A WEAPON!

YOU HAVE UNLOCKED THE SECRET OF THE TEMPLE. HOW DID *YOU* ACCOMPLISH THIS?

YOU'RE SMART, FIGURE IT OUT!

KRSSZ

NO MATTER, THE POWER WITHIN WILL SOON SERVE THE EMPEROR.

I DON'T FEAR YOU!

THEN YOU WILL DIE BRAVER THAN MOST.

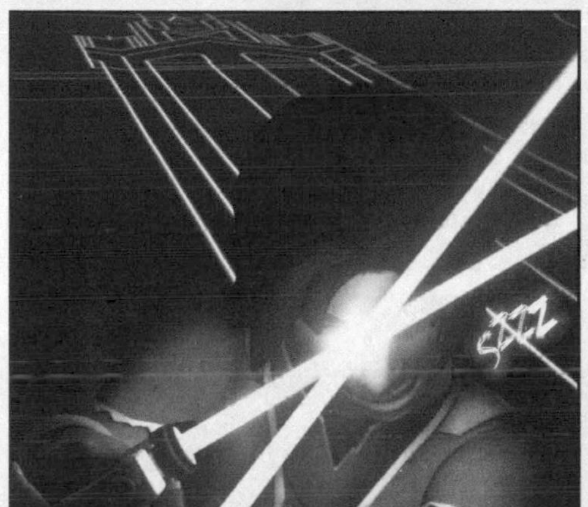
SZZZ

UGH.

AAH!
KRKTCHAK

WHUD

PERHAPS
I WAS
WRONG.

IT WOULDN'T BE
THE FIRST TIME.

IT WAS
FORETOLD THAT
YOU WOULD BE HERE.
OUR LONG-AWAITED
MEETING HAS COME
AT LAST.

I'M GLAD I GAVE
YOU SOMETHING TO
LOOK FORWARD TO.
WE NEED NOT BE
ADVERSARIES.

THE EMPEROR WILL SHOW YOU MERCY IF YOU TELL ME WHERE THE REMAINING JEDI CAN BE FOUND.

THERE ARE NO JEDI. YOU AND YOUR INQUISITORS HAVE SEEN TO THAT.

PERHAPS THIS CHILD WILL CONFESS WHAT YOU WILL NOT.

I WAS BEGINNING TO BELIEVE I KNEW WHO YOU WERE BEHIND THAT MASK, BUT IT'S IMPOSSIBLE.
MY MASTER COULD *NEVER* BE AS VILE AS YOU.

ANAKIN SKYWALKER WAS WEAK. I DESTROYED HIM.

THEN I WILL *AVENGE* HIS DEATH.

REVENGE IS NOT THE JEDI WAY.

I AM NO JEDI.

TSSSHEW

TSSSHEW

STZZZ

I NEED A LOT MORE TRAINING.
THE HOLOCRON!

CRZZZ

I CAN'T LET HIM GET IT.

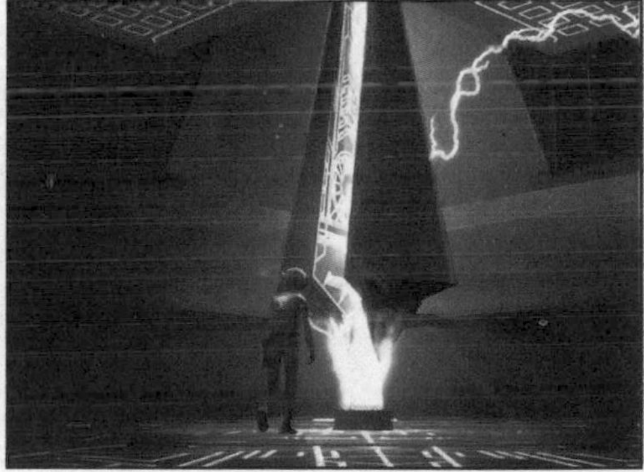

RRGH. AHH!

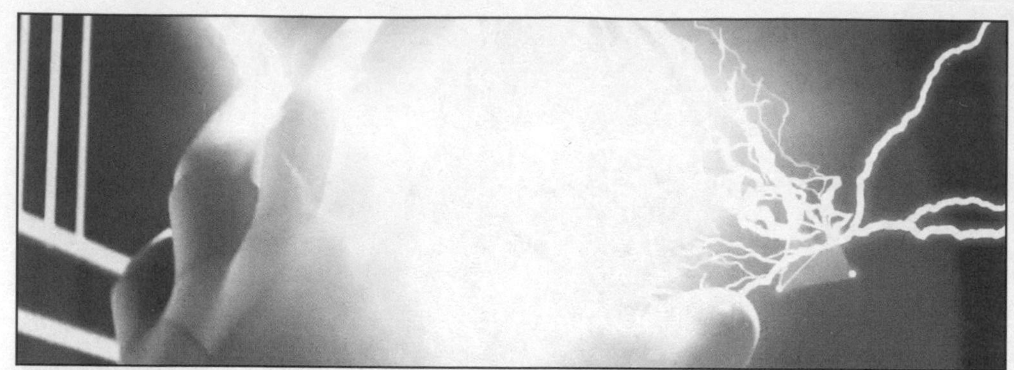

BLAM
UGH.

IT TAKES A MASTER *AND* AN APPRENTICE.

KANAN! WAIT, WHAT HAPPENED, WHY ARE YOU WEARING THAT?
I'LL EXPLAIN LATER. CHOPPER, GET THE *PHANTOM* READY.

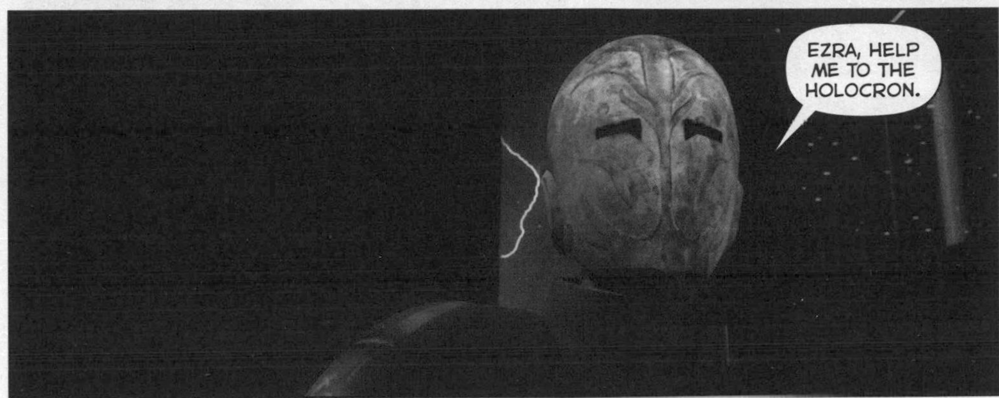
EZRA, HELP ME TO THE HOLOCRON.

KANAN, YOUR EYES...

LET'S WORRY ABOUT THAT LATER. WE'VE GOT TO GET THAT HOLOCRON OUT OF HERE. WHERE'S AHSOKA?

SIGH
WITH VADER.

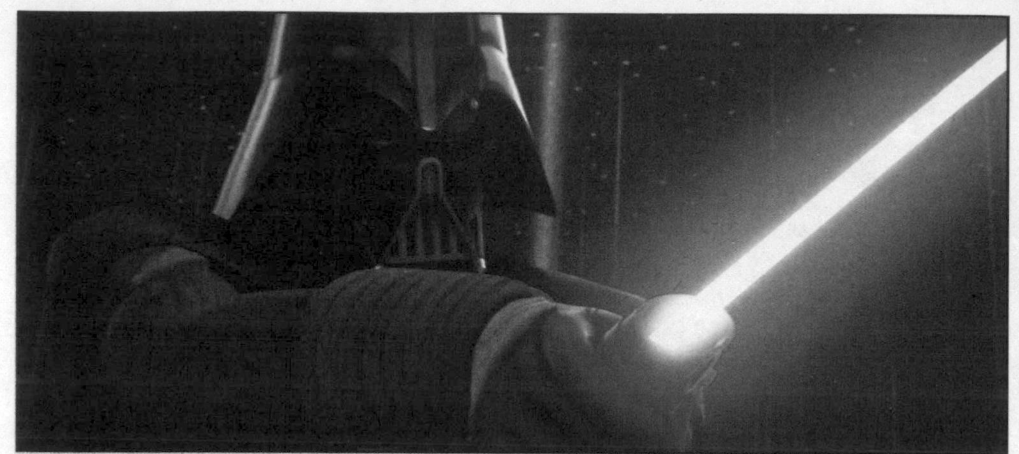

KTCHAK

ZZRT

SZZZ

ZRAAAK

UGH--
AARGH!

A FEW MORE STEPS.

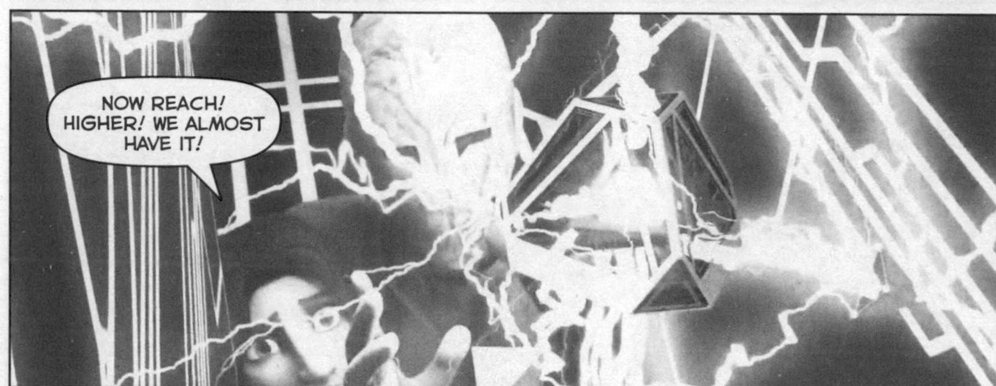
NOW REACH! HIGHER! WE ALMOST HAVE IT!

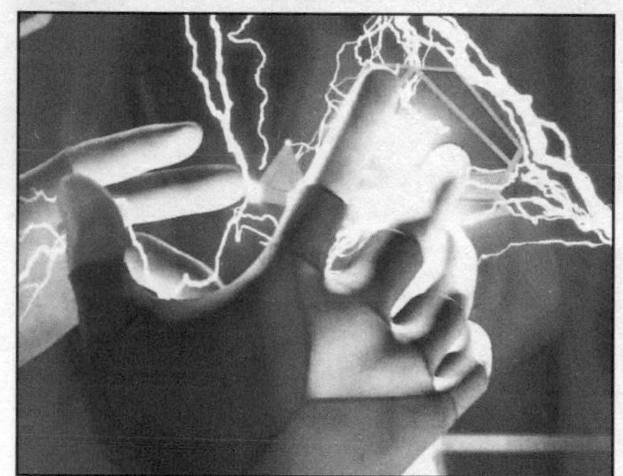

FZZZZZ

NOW PULL!

AUGH!
BLAM
AHHH!

RRRRRRRR
THE TEMPLE'S STARTING TO COLLAPSE!

ZKRRRRRZZ

WHUP BUP
BUP WHUP

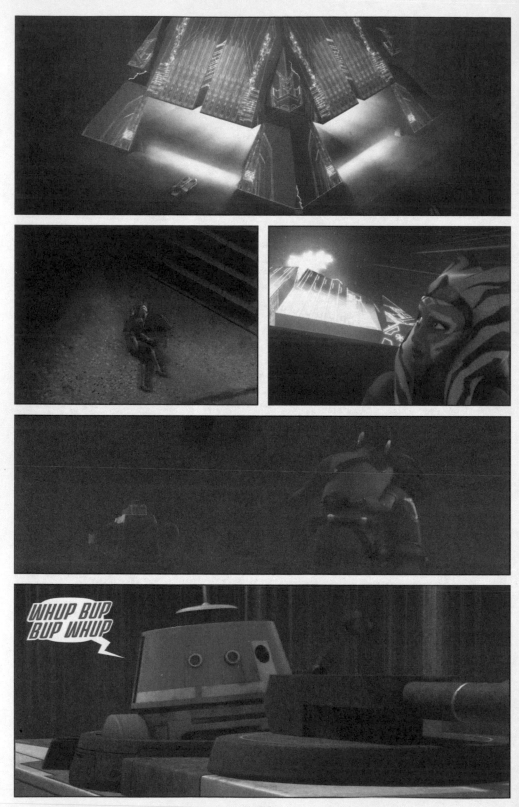

WE'RE COMING AS FAST AS WE CAN! JUST BE READY TO GO--

WHOA! WHOA! WHOA! NO! NO, NO, NO, NO, NO, NO, NO, NO, NO!

KANAN! IT'S HIM!

I KNOW! I GOT YOU!

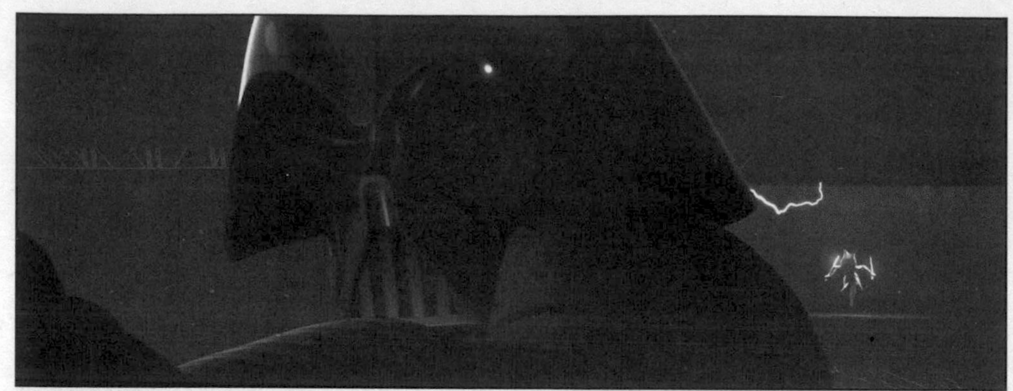

AAGH!
VTRZZ
AHHH--

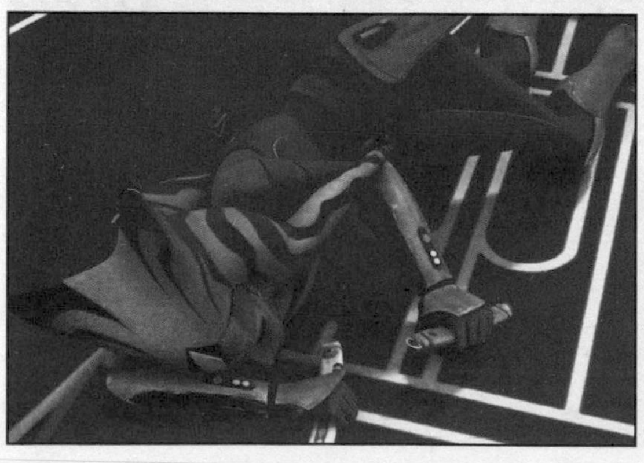

AHSOKA! COME ON, HURRY!

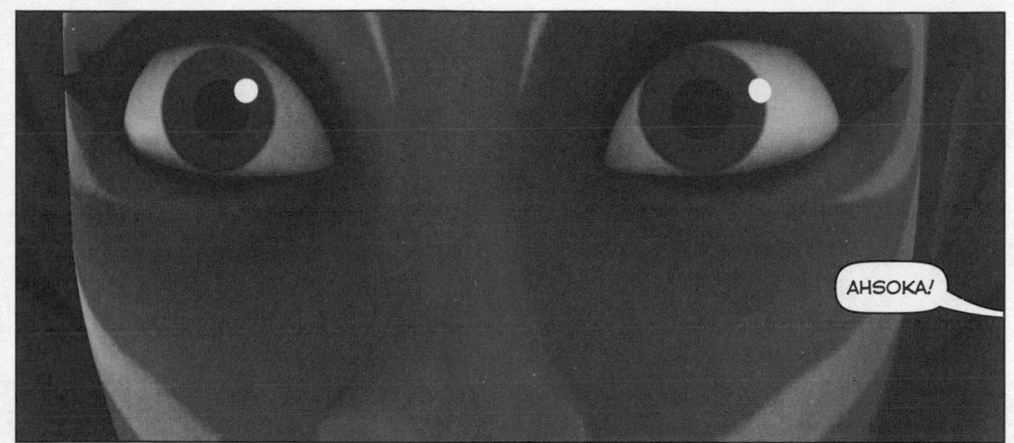
AHSOKA!

AHSOKA.

ANAKIN.

I WON'T LEAVE YOU. *NOT THIS TIME.*

THEN YOU WILL *DIE.*

AHSOKA!

NO!
NO!

EZRA!
EZRA, LET'S GO!

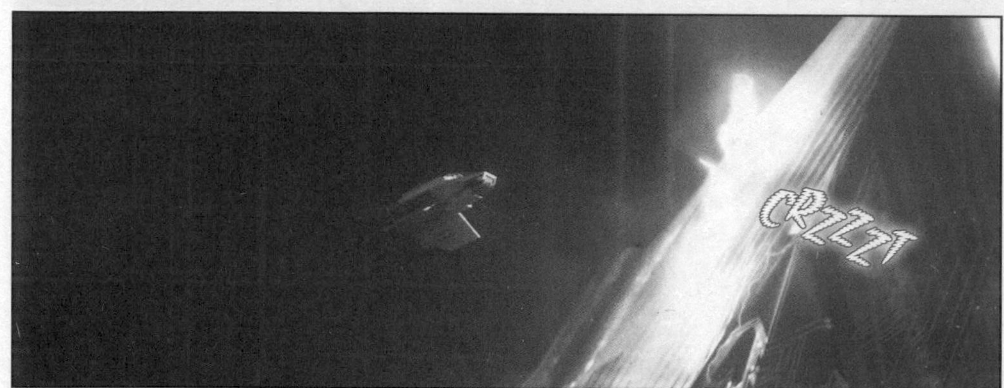
CRZZZT

KATHOOOM

SHOOM

THE PHANTOM.

THERE'S NOTHING WE CAN DO NOW, IT'S OVER. IT'S OVER.

SOB

CHOPPER BASE, ATOLLON.

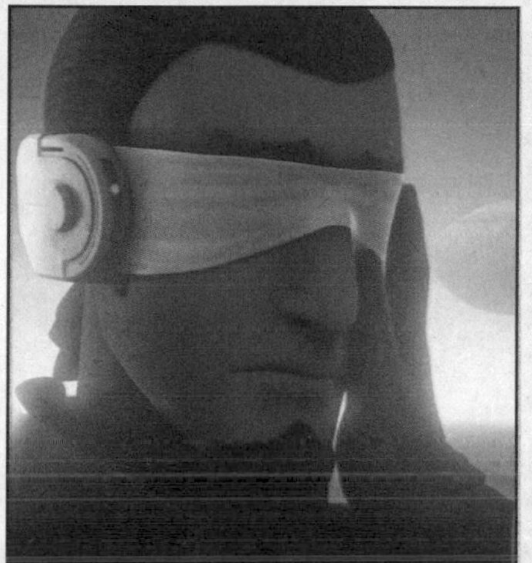

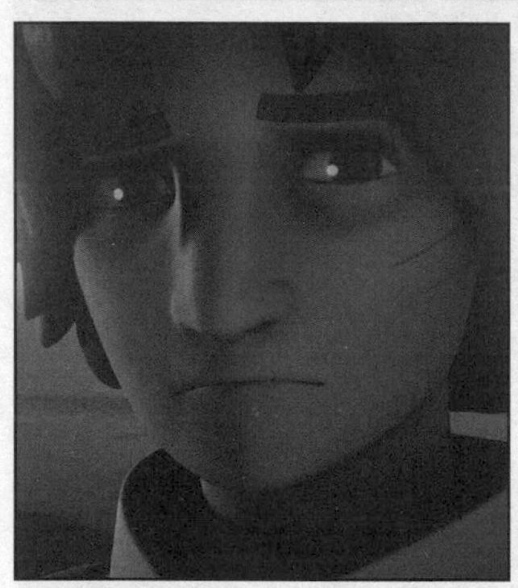

SPACE ABOVE MALACHOR.

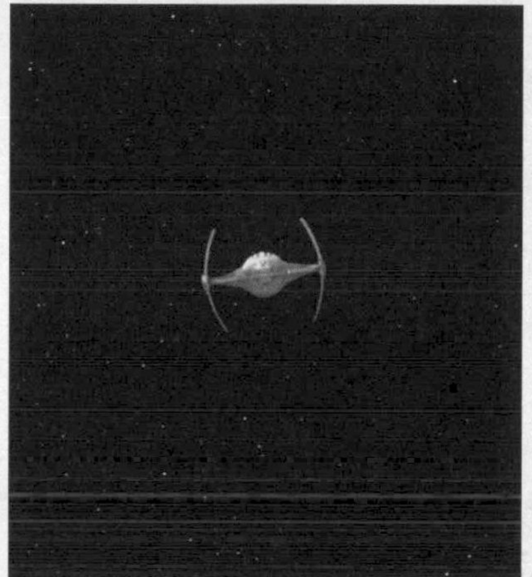

MALACHOR--SURFACE.

THE GHOST.

THE HOLOCRONS OF FATE

CR90 CORVETTE,
HYPERSPACE.

YOU'RE NOT GONNA TELL ME WHAT YOU DID WITH THE SITH HOLOCRON, ARE YOU?
I TOLD YOU IT WAS *SAFE.*

BUT WHAT IF THERE ARE SECRETS WE CAN LEARN FROM IT THAT'LL HELP US DESTROY THE SITH?

EZRA, THE SECRETS IN THAT THING ALMOST DESTROYED *YOU.*

I KNOW, BUT IF NOT TO GET THE SITH HOLOCRON, WHY DID MASTER YODA SEND US TO MALACHOR?

WE ASKED FOR A CHANCE TO DEFEAT THE SITH. AND WE FAILED.

WE'RE COMING UP ON THE RENDEZVOUS POINT, COMMANDER...

...BUT THE TRANSPORT'S NOT RESPONDING.

LOOKS LIKE IT WAS ATTACKED.

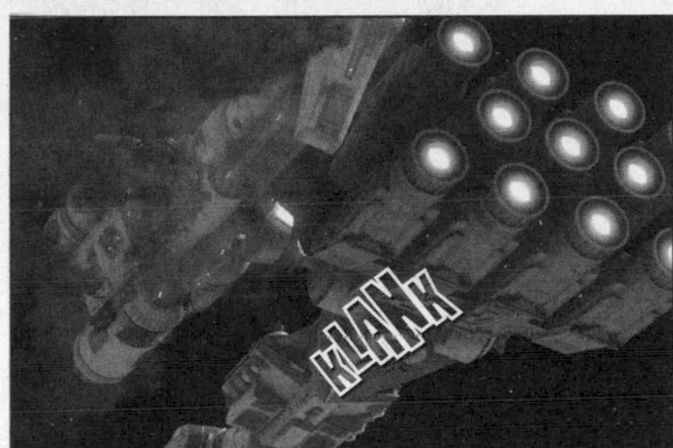
KLANK

THERE MUST HAVE BEEN ONE HECK OF A FIGHT.

I CAN SMELL THE CARBON SCORING.
BRRRP BEEP WUURRRP

OVER HERE.

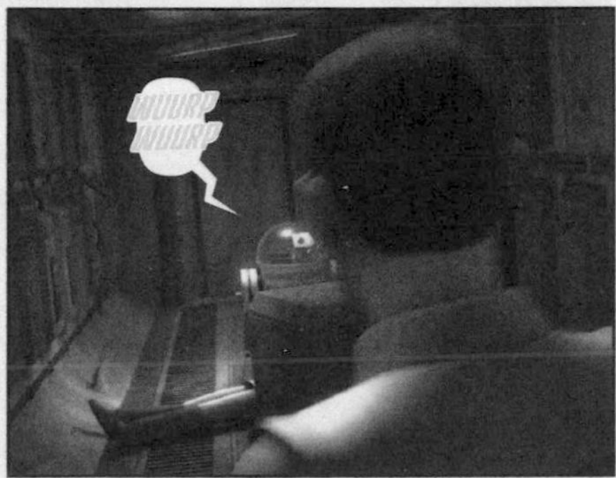
WUURP WUURP

UGH...

HANG ON, ALL RIGHT? WE'LL GET YOU HELP. WHAT HAPPENED HERE?

RED...RED BLADE... AFTER YOU...MADE ME TELL...THE *GHOST* IS IN DANGER. *ARGH...*

ANOTHER INQUISITOR?

WE'VE GOTTA WARN HERA.

GOT THE *GHOST* FOR YOU NOW, SIR.

HERA! AM I GLAD TO SEE YOU'RE ALL RIGHT.

KANAN.

THERE'S ANOTHER INQUISITOR AFTER US. HE KNOWS WHERE THE *GHOST* IS.

KANAN, IT'S NOT AN INQUISITOR.

JUST AN OLD FRIEND, MASTER JEDI.

MAUL? YOU BETRAYED ME!

NO, I BETRAYED YOUR FRIEND. BUT I WOULD HAVE REMAINED LOYAL TO YOU.

WHAT DO YOU WANT?

THE SITH HOLOCRON THAT OUR APPRENTICE AND I ACQUIRED ON MALACHOR.

WE DON'T HAVE IT.

HOW UNFORTUNATE, BECAUSE IF THAT'S TRUE...THEN YOUR FRIENDS HAVE NO FUTURE.
TSSSHEW

OKAY, WE HAVE IT--JUST NOT *WITH* US.

WE'LL GIVE IT TO YOU, AS LONG AS OUR FRIENDS REMAIN SAFE.

AGREED. GOOD. OH, AND ONE MORE THING-- YOUR **JEDI HOLOCRON...** GIVE THAT TO ME AS WELL.

KANAN, NO.

FINE.

I SHALL BE IN TOUCH WITH COORDINATES FOR OUR RENDEZVOUS. DON'T DISAPPOINT ME.

I CAN'T BELIEVE YOU TOLD MAUL I HAVE A HOLOCRON.

AT THE TIME, HE WAS ON *OUR* SIDE. IS IT STILL ON THE *GHOST?*

WHERE ELSE WOULD I KEEP IT?

WELL, WHAT ABOUT THE SITH HOLOCRON?

YEAH...THAT'S NOT GONNA BE EASY.
I THOUGHT YOU SAID IT WAS SAFE.
IT IS SAFE-- THAT MAY BE THE PROBLEM.

MEANWHILE, ON THE GHOST.

I ASSUMED THAT THIS SHIP WAS MERELY A TRANSPORT, BUT I REALIZE IT IS MUCH MORE THAN THAT...
...THIS IS YOUR *HOME*.

YOU LOOKIN' TO MOVE IN?

CAPTAIN, WOULD IT BE RUDE OF ME TO REQUEST A TOUR OF YOUR SHIP?

WELL, THE AIRLOCK IS DOWN THERE, IF YOU WANT TO SEE YOURSELF OUT.

SHOW ME
AROUND. I
INSIST.

NO!

HERA,
DON'T!
ARRRGH!

MANDALORIAN, YOU
OF ALL SHOULD TRUST
ME. FOR DID I NOT ONCE
RULE YOUR PEOPLE?

IS THAT TRUE?
UNFORTUNATELY.

WHERE DOES ONE WHO HIDES HIS IDENTITY, HIDE HIS LEGACY?

-SNIFF- THAT IS A CURIOUS SMELL.

A DULL AND DOUR CHAMBER. THESE ARE THE QUARTERS OF A JEDI.

SHOW ME WHERE HE KEEPS THE HOLOCRON.

I DON'T KNOW ANYTHING ABOUT HIM.

THAT'S NOT TRUE--YOU KNOW ALL ABOUT KANAN JARRUS. OR SHOULD I USE HIS REAL NAME? CALEB DUME.

GASP

YES...IT WAS *YOUR* IDEA TO RECRUIT THE APPRENTICE. AND IT WAS FROM HERE THAT THE BOY FOUND...

...GASP NO, HE *STOLE* THE HOLOCRON.

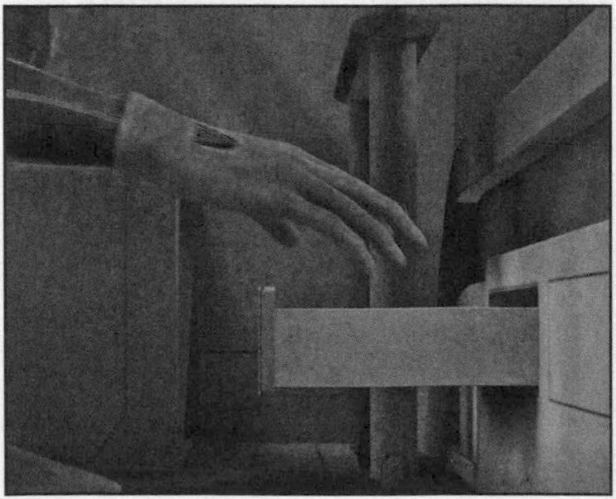

MM-HMM-HA-HA-HA!
THAT WASN'T SO DIFFICULT, WAS IT?

ATOLLON.

SO, YOU HID THE HOLOCRON DOWN THERE?

MORE LIKE... I LEFT IT WITH SOMEONE.

SOMEONE? WHO?

BENDU? BENDU,
ARE YOU HERE?

BENDU? WHO'S BENDU?
THERE'S NOTHING HERE.

HE WAS HERE...

MAYBE YOU'RE JUST HEARING THINGS THAT AREN'T THERE.

BENDU! I NEED THE HOLOCRON! BENDU!

MMM, KANAN, I DON'T SEE YOUR FRIEND.

GASP OH! OH, BUT I DO SEE CRAWLERS!

LOTS OF 'EM! HEY, WHERE'S OUR THUMPER?

HISS

IF YOU STAY CALM, THEY WON'T ATTACK.

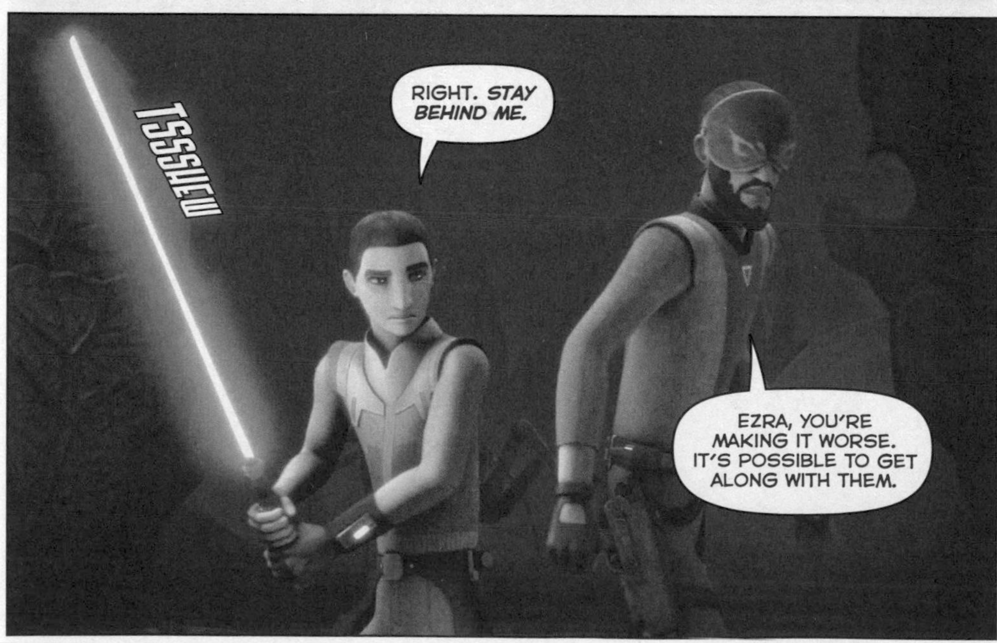
TSSSHEW
RIGHT. *STAY BEHIND ME.*
EZRA, YOU'RE MAKING IT WORSE. IT'S POSSIBLE TO GET ALONG WITH THEM.

MMM...I TRIED THAT, REMEMBER? THEY ALMOST RIPPED MY FACE OFF.

RKLLLK

HE'S HERE.

WHAT?

RRRRRRR

GRRRRMMM...

THE JEDI RETURNS WITH HIS STUDENT.

PERHAPS FOR A TALK? HA-HA-HA-HA-HA.

I DON'T BELIEVE IT!

UNFORTUNATELY, WE DON'T HAVE TIME TO CHAT, BENDU. WE'VE COME FOR THE HOLOCRON.

AH, YES,
THE KEEPER OF THE
SHADOW LORE. WHY DO
YOU WANT IT?

TELL HIM,
EZRA.

OKAY.
WE NEED IT TO
SAVE OUR FRIENDS.
A SITH, DARTH MAUL,
HAS THEM. HE
WANTS IT.

I DO NOT KNOW
THIS DARK SIDER, BUT
I KNOW HIS KIND. WHY
DOES HE WANT IT?

I DON'T KNOW. BUT HE ALSO WANTS MY JEDI HOLOCRON.

OH. HE WOULD BRING THEM TOGETHER? SUCH A VERGENCE CARRIES *GRAVE DANGER.*

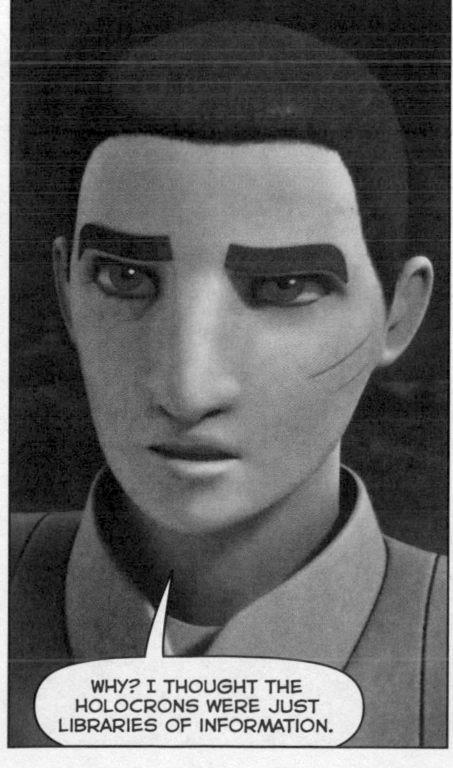
WHY? I THOUGHT THE HOLOCRONS WERE JUST LIBRARIES OF INFORMATION.

THEY ARE THAT AND *MORE.* IF TWO SUCH POWERFUL SOURCES OF KNOWLEDGE ARE UNITED, THEY WILL GRANT A CLARITY OF VISION *BEYOND* YOUR KIND.

WHAT DOES THAT MEAN?

WHEN JOINED, ANY SECRET, WISDOM, OR DESTINY CAN BE SEEN THROUGH THE FORCE. ONE COULD BRING MUCH CHAOS WITH SUCH HIDDEN TRUTHS.
I HAVE SEEN IT BEFORE.

WELL, WE CAN'T CONTROL WHAT MAUL WILL DO.
THAT'S HIS POINT, EZRA.

WELL, WE STILL NEED IT TO SAVE OUR FRIENDS, KANAN.
SO, ARE YOU GONNA GIVE IT BACK, OR NOT?

HMM. THE OBJECT YOU SEEK IS A SOURCE OF IMBALANCE BETWEEN YOU AND YOUR TEACHER.
IF YOU WANT IT, YOU MUST SEEK IT OUT WITH HIM.

WHERE IS IT?

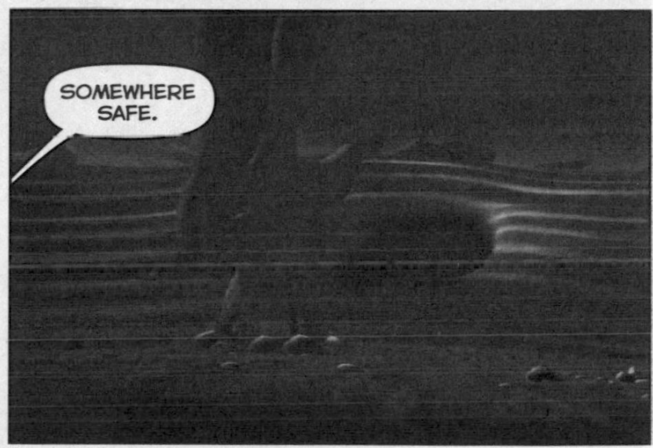
SOMEWHERE SAFE.

ALL RIGHT, I'LL GO, BUT I'M GOING ALONE.

THE CAVE RUNS DEEP, WITH MANY TWISTS AND TURNS...HOW CAN YOU BE SURE WHERE IT IS NOW? HMM?

I HEAR SOMETHING.

IF YOU LISTEN, YOU CAN HEAR IT.

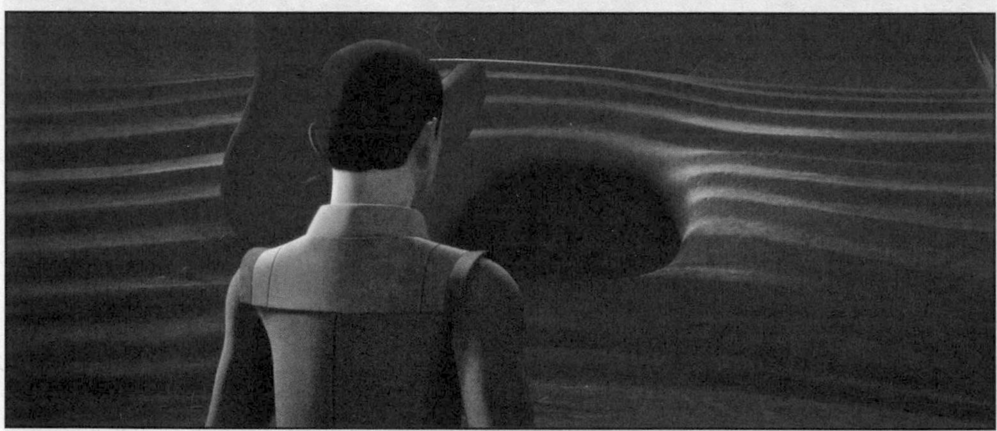

I'LL HOLD ON TO THIS.
KANAN! THE SPIDERS--
--WILL ATTACK AS SOON AS YOU TURN IT ON. USE YOUR COMLINK INSTEAD. I'LL TRY TO GUIDE YOU FROM HERE.

-SIGH- I'D RATHER HAVE MY LIGHTSABER.
WHY TAKE HIS WEAPON? 
HE'S GOTTA LEARN HOW TO SOLVE PROBLEMS WITHOUT IT.

BACK ON THE GHOST.

YOU WILL *YIELD* TO MY POWER. *ARGH.*

AARRGHH!

WOW. SOMEONE'S NOT HAPPY.

WHUP WHUP BUHBUH BUHHH

KRRSH

AARGH!

KRASH

SMSSH

GET TO THE ENGINE ROOM, QUIETLY.

CLANK

THUNK THUNK

HERE HE COMES--
HE MAKES AN AWFUL
LOT OF CLANKING.

HE *IS* PART
DROID.

WE CAN USE THAT
AGAINST HIM.

THUNK
THUNK

HE'S IN THE HOLD.

CHOPPER, MAGNETIZE!

WHUH BUP

!

THUD

TSSSHEW

PTHEW

TZZZT

WHUMP

AUGH.
AGH.

FWOOSH
UGH.

FSSH

YOU WILL REMAIN ALIVE...

...ONLY SO LONG AS YOU'RE OF USE TO ME!

BACK ON ATOLLON.

EZRA, KEEP TO THE LEFT.

LEFT? YOU SURE ABOUT THAT?
TRUST ME.

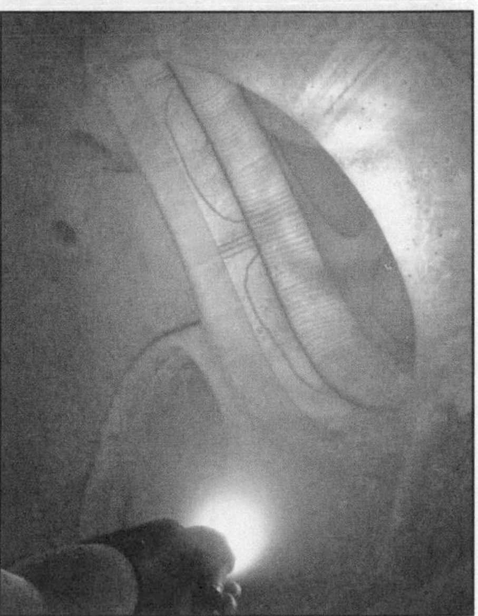

HHHK
GASP
EZRA! WHAT'S HAPPENING?!

EZRA? EZRA!

KEEP AN EYE ON THOSE, WILL YA?

PERHAPS MASTER AND APPRENTICE WILL REDISCOVER THEIR BALANCE.

PRRP PEEP

OR PERHAPS THEY'LL BE EATEN. SUCH IS THE WAY OF THINGS.

UNGH!

UGH.
HISSS

EZRA, JUMP!

UNGH

WHAT ARE YOU *DOING* IN HERE?

GETTING YOU BACK ON TRACK.

HOW DID YOU DO THAT?
I CAN'T EVEN DO THAT.

WELL, I'VE BEEN FORCED
TO SEE THINGS DIFFERENTLY
SINCE MALACHOR.

ABOUT WHAT HAPPENED... I'M SORRY FOR IT. FOR EVERYTHING, KANAN.

IT WASN'T YOUR FAULT.
I NEVER BLAMED YOU, EZRA. IT'S TIME FOR YOU TO FORGIVE YOURSELF.

YES, MASTER.

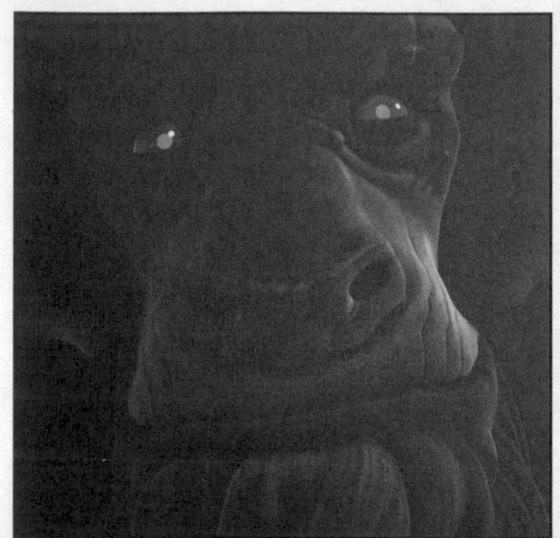

THERE IT IS.

STAY CALM.

STEADY...

FWOOSH

KANAN...

DON'T BE
A THREAT.

GO IN
PEACE.

YOUR CONFLICT HAS ENDED--PERHAPS BALANCE IS RESTORED.

THANKS, BENDU.

YOUR TRUE STRUGGLE HAS ONLY *BEGUN.*

BE WARNED--THE DARK SIDER WILL NOT BE ABLE TO OPEN YOUR JEDI HOLOCRON.

THAT TASK WILL FALL TO ONE OF YOU.

SO THAT MEANS WE'LL HAVE THE POWER OF BOTH HOLOCRONS TOO.

DO WHAT YOU MUST, BUT SUCH POWER COMES WITH A PRICE.
ONCE A SECRET IS KNOWN, IT CANNOT BE *UNKNOWN.*

LATER, RZ-1T STARSHIP, HYPERSPACE.

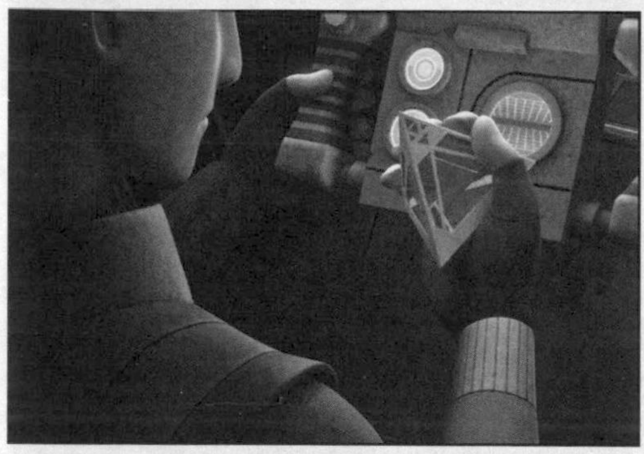

YOU WANTED IT, NOW YOU GOT IT.

IF YOU REALLY THINK IT'LL HELP US AGAINST MAUL, OPEN IT UP.

I'D RATHER HEAR WHAT YOU HAVE TO SAY. WHAT'S OUR PLAN?

I THINK WE OUGHTA PLAY IT BY EAR.

HOW CAN YOU TAKE THIS LIGHTLY?

YEAH, WELL, I *LOOK* RELAXED.

MANDALORIAN
ASTEROID BASE.
SHMMMM

OVER HERE,
MASTER JEDI.

JUST FOLLOW
THE SOUND OF
MY VOICE.

EASY.

WELCOME, MY YOUNG APPRENTICE. I TRUST YOU FOUND THE SITH HOLOCRON... *ILLUMINATING?*

I DON'T SEE OUR FRIENDS.

THEY WILL REMAIN MY *GUESTS* UNTIL WE CONCLUDE OUR BUSINESS. I WILL TAKE YOU TO THEM NOW.

ESCORT MY APPRENTICE TO THE COMMAND CENTER.
IF YOU ATTEMPT TO ESCAPE, OR IF THE DROIDS ARE DEACTIVATED...YOUR FRIENDS WILL DIE.

GOOD TO KNOW.

THIS WAY, *MASTER JEDI.*

TRUTHFULLY, I WAS NEVER TRYING TO BLIND YOU.

OH, NO. YOU WERE JUST TRYING TO *KILL* ME.

WELL, IF AT FIRST YOU DON'T SUCCEED--

HEY!

--*TRY, TRY AGAIN.*

WHSSSH

AAGH!

NO!

WHSSSH

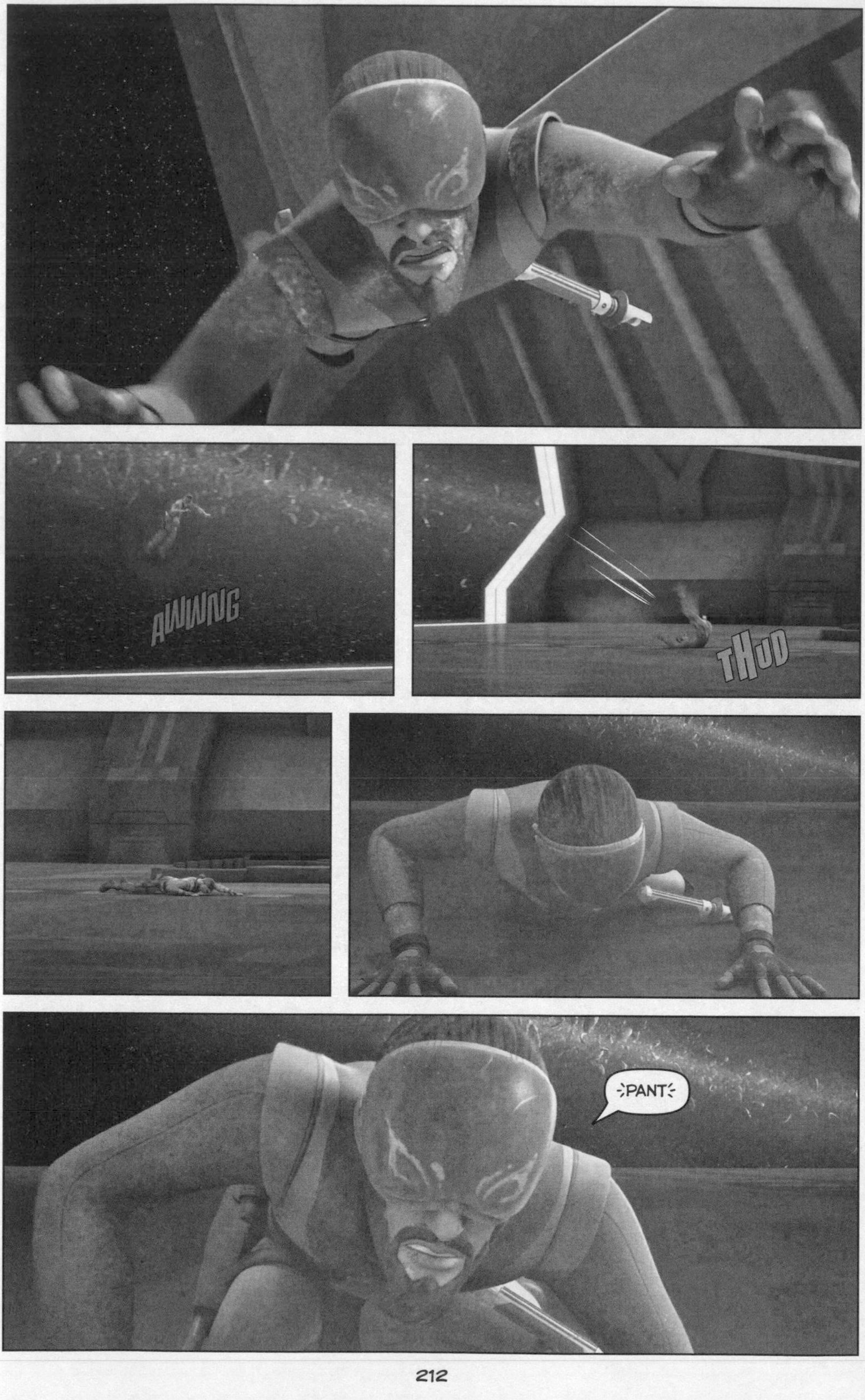

AWWNG

THUD

TERMINATE THE PRISONERS.

I LIVED UP TO MY END OF THE BARGAIN, YOUR FRIENDS ARE SAFE.
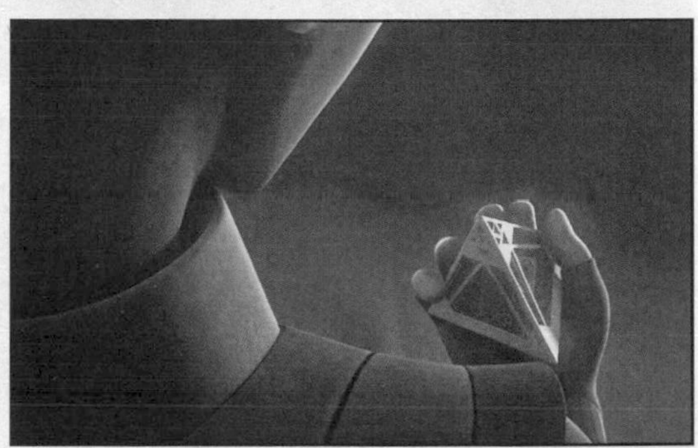

COME, APPRENTICE, SIT.

THE HOLOCRON, IF YOU PLEASE.

I DOUBT THAT YOU COMPREHEND THE *POWER* THAT IS WITHIN YOUR GRASP.

I KNOW IF WE OPEN THESE HOLOCRONS TOGETHER, ANY QUESTION WE ASK WILL BE ANSWERED.

SO YOU *DO* UNDERSTAND. WELL, MY APPRENTICE, WHAT IS YOUR QUESTION?

YOU KNOW WHAT I WANT-- I WANT TO DESTROY THE SITH.

YOU ARE AS AMBITIOUS AS EVER.
AS FOR ME, I SEEK SOMETHING MUCH SIMPLER, YET EQUALLY ELUSIVE.

WHAT'S THAT?

HOPE.

NOW, LET US BEGIN.

STTTTTZZZZZ

THOOM

MEANWHILE, ON THE GHOST...

VRRP
WRRP

WHERE'S EZRA?

WITH MAUL. *LET'S GO.*

WHUH BUHBUP

I SEE NOTHING. ONLY OBLIVION. I MUST GO DEEPER. GO DEEPER!

WAIT, I SEE SOMETHING.

WHAT DO YOU SEE? WHAT IS IT?

I SEE...

TELL ME! TELL ME WHAT YOU SEE!

I SEE...

EZRA!
WHOOOM

AH--IT'S TOO BRIGHT!
WHERE IS HE?

EZRA.
I SEE HIM! MAUL'S CLOSE. I'M GOING TO GET EZRA OUT. BE READY.

WAIT. YOU SEE HIM?

KANAN!

EZRA. EZRA, LISTEN TO ME! LOOK AWAY!
KANAN?

NO! STAY FOCUSED, APPRENTICE. GAIN THE KNOWLEDGE YOU DESIRE.

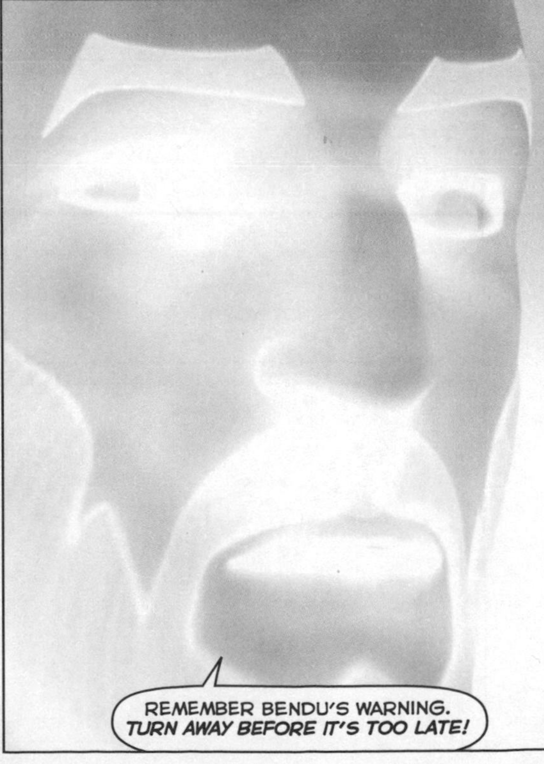
REMEMBER BENDU'S WARNING. TURN AWAY BEFORE IT'S TOO LATE!

BUT IT'S SO CLOSE...THE KEY TO DESTROYING THE SITH. JUST A LITTLE FURTHER.

I SEE HIM.
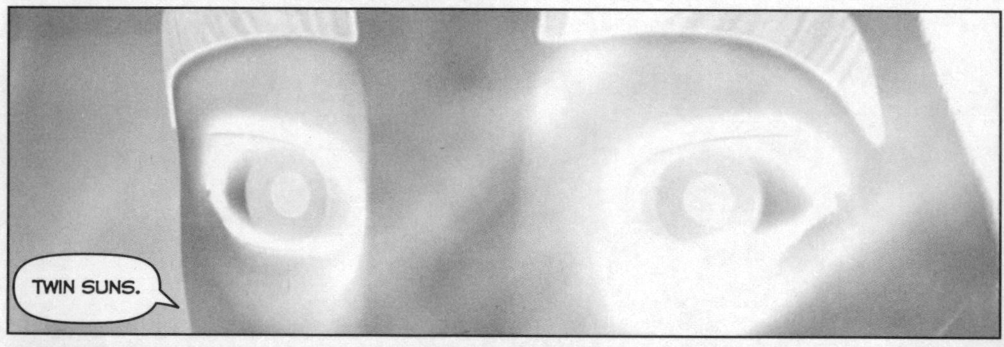
TWIN SUNS.

IT'S NOT WORTH IT, EZRA. TRUST ME.

TZZZZ

NO!

KATHOOM

UGH. WHERE'S MAUL?

HE LIVES.

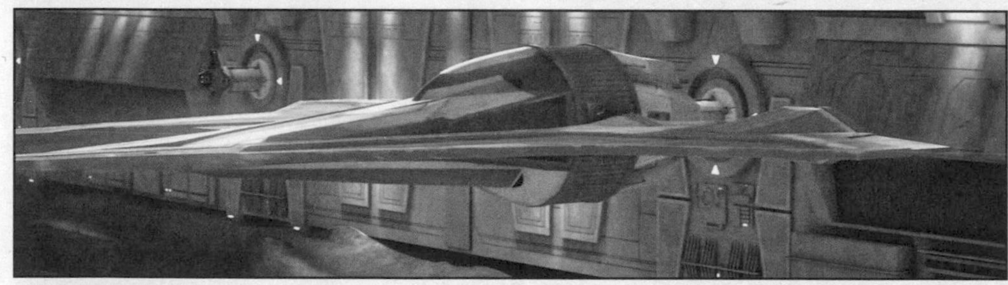

HA-HA! HE LIVES.

HA-HA-HA!

COME ON, FIND YOUR WAY OUT, EZRA.

COME BACK TO US.

RRGGH.

YOU OKAY, KID?

UGH, I THINK SO. KANAN, YOU...YOU CAN SEE AGAIN? Y-YOU CAN SEE ME?

I COULD, BUT ONLY THROUGH THE LIGHT OF THE HOLOCRONS. DO YOU KNOW WHAT HAPPENED?

I SAW IMAGES, PIECES OF SOMETHING, BUT I CAN'T MAKE SENSE OF 'EM.
I DON'T KNOW IF IT'S WHAT I WANTED TO SEE, OR WHAT MAUL WAS TRYING TO SEE.

WHAT WERE THEY?

PLACES, MOSTLY. PLANETS. SOME FAMILIAR...SOME NOT. I'M NOT SURE WHAT THEY MEAN.

I'M SURE WE'LL FIND OUT TOGETHER.

VISIONS & VOICES

CHOPPER BASE--
ATOLLON.

EVEN THOUGH WE STILL HAVE SOME PREPARATION TO DO BEFORE WE STRIKE THE EMPIRE'S FACTORY ON LOTHAL...

EZRA.

...I WANT TO DO A THOROUGH RECON TRIP TO UPDATE OUR INTEL. THERE'S NO NEED FOR THE FULL SQUADRON, A SMALL UNIT SHOULD BE ABLE TO HANDLE THIS.

EZRA.

I'M ASSIGNING YOU THE MISSION, EZRA.

EZRA.

EZRA?
GASP

CARE TO JOIN THE BRIEFING?

SORRY. YEAH. NO, IT'S JUST, I THOUGHT I SAW SOMETHING.

THIS IS YOUR MISSION, EZRA. I NEED YOUR *FULL* ATTENTION.

YEAH, YOU'VE GOT IT. SORRY.

ALL RIGHT. SO FIRST, YOU'LL SLIP INTO THE SYSTEM AND STUDY THE EMPIRE'S ORBITAL DEFENSES.

EZRA.

WE'LL KEEP OUR DISTANCE, BUT GATHER ALL THE DATA WE CAN. I WANT DESTROYER POSITIONS, TIE PATROL ROUTES, TRANSPORT SCHEDULES--

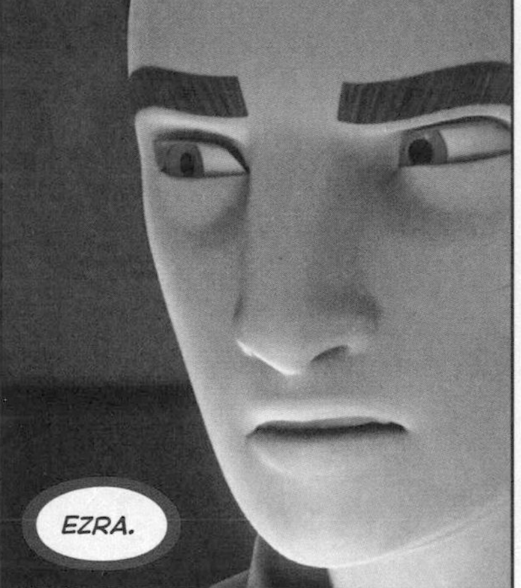
EZRA.

GASP

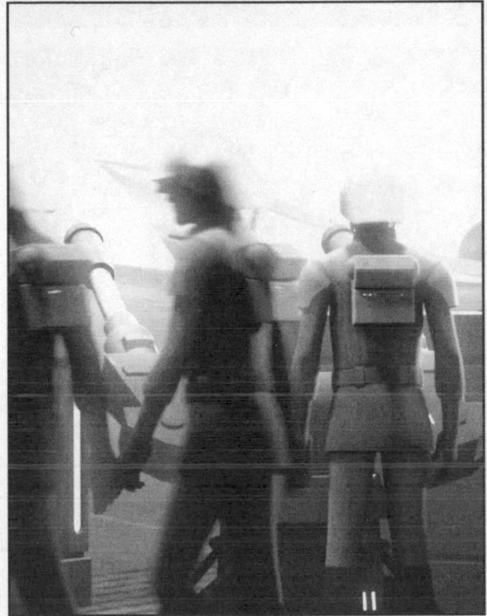

SOMETHING WRONG?

NO, I JUST...I THOUGHT I SAW SOMETHING, OR SOMEONE.

THE RECON TEAM LEAVES AS SOON AS WE'RE LOADED UP. QUESTIONS?

IS ADMIRAL THRAWN THERE?

WE HAVE REPORTS OF AN INCREASE IN CAPITAL SHIPS, BUT NO CONFIRMATION AS TO WHETHER HE'S THERE OR NOT.

EZRA...

HEY, KID.
YOU FEELIN' ALL
RIGHT?

THERE!
LOOK!

WHAT AM
I LOOKING
AT?

YOU DON'T
LOOK VERY
GOOD.

EZRA,
WHAT DO YOU
SEE?

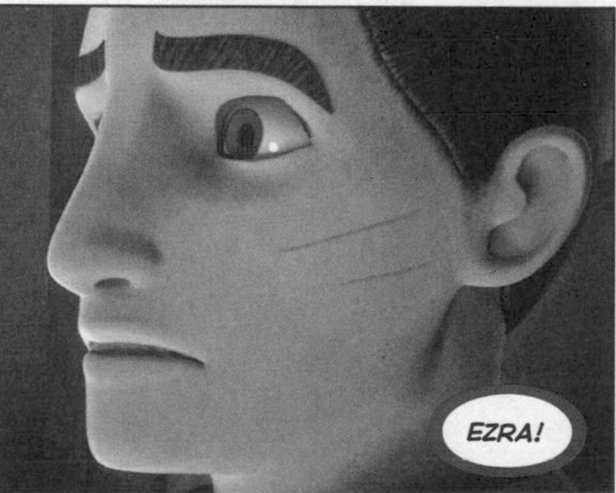
EZRA!

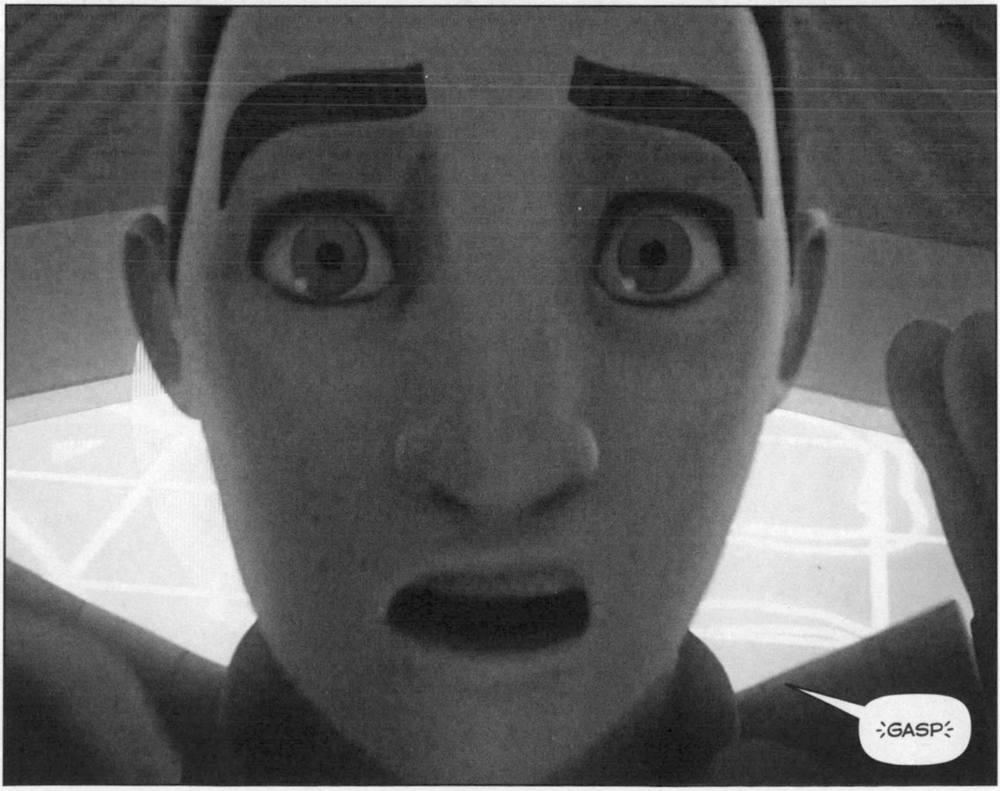

GASP

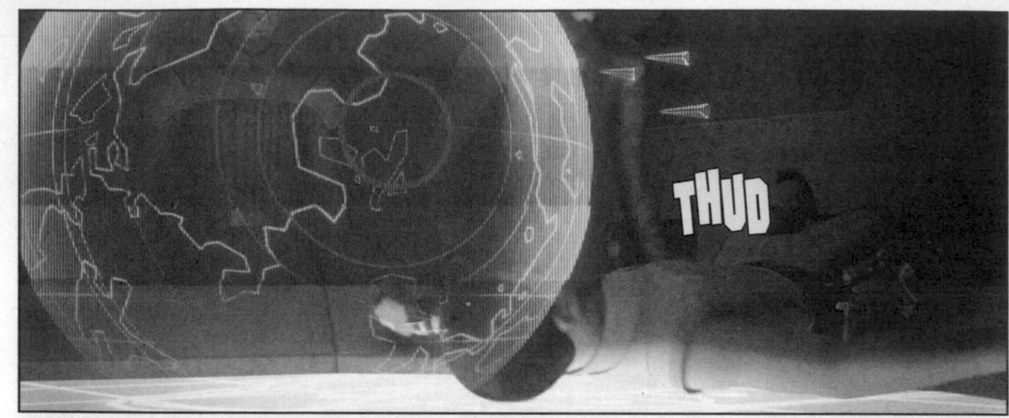
THUD

EZRA!

KANAN, WHAT'S GOING ON?

I DON'T KNOW. *I DON'T KNOW!*
EZRA, CAN YOU HEAR ME? *EZRA!*

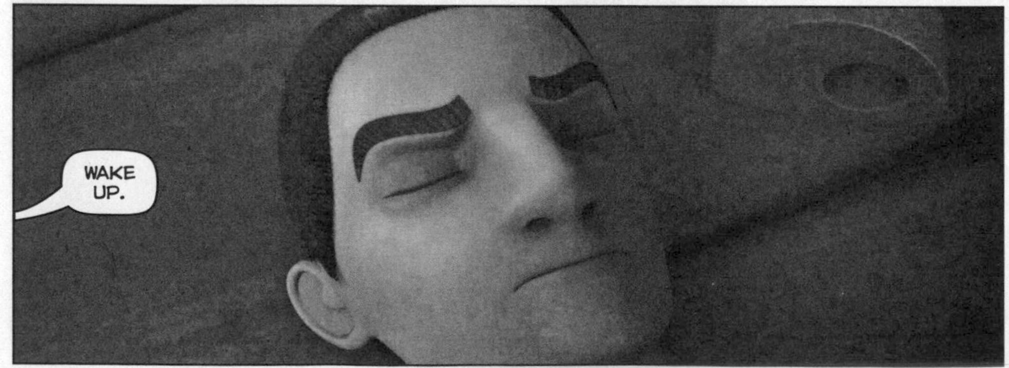
WAKE UP.

-GASP-

WHOA, EZRA. IT'S OKAY, YOU'RE SAFE.

YOU WANT TO TELL US WHAT'S GOING ON?

IT WAS *MAUL.*

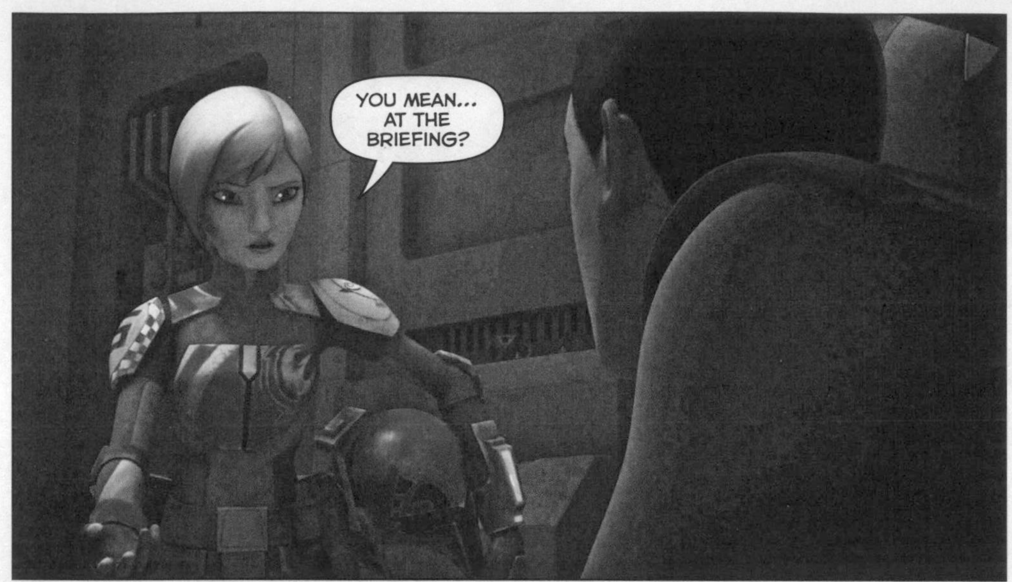
YOU MEAN...
AT THE
BRIEFING?

I SAW HIM.
HE SAID MY NAME.
HE WAS RIGHT BEHIND
ME. I MEAN, HE WAS
RIGHT THERE.

KID, I WAS STANDING
NEXT TO YOU. THERE WAS
NOBODY ELSE THERE.

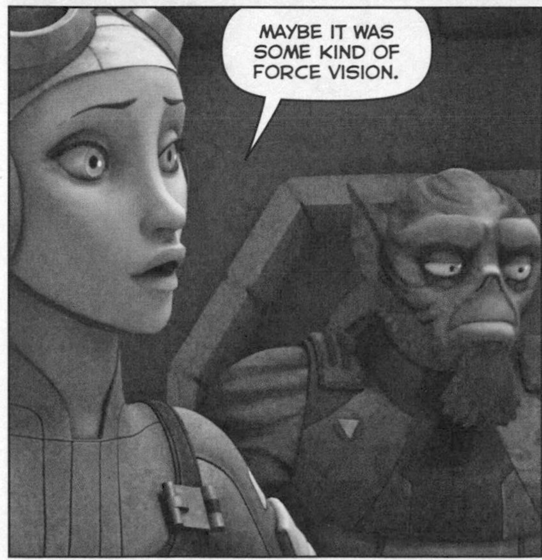
MAYBE IT WAS
SOME KIND OF
FORCE VISION.

MMM,
MAYBE.

AH, IF YOU ASK ME, THE KID'S JUST BEEN WORKING TOO HARD.

WHUH BUHBUH BUH BUP

CHOPPER, STOP IT.
BUH BUP

NO, CHOP'S RIGHT, NAP TIME'S OVER. I SHOULD GET BACK TO WORK.

YOU SURE YOU'RE ALL RIGHT?

HERA, *I FEEL FINE.* I JUST HAD A BAD... SOMETHING.

NO REASON TO STOP THE REBELLION, RIGHT? COME ON, SABINE. WE GOTTA GET READY FOR OUR MISSION.

TELL ME WHAT YOU'RE THINKING, KANAN.

I'M THINKING WHATEVER EZRA WENT THROUGH WITH MAUL...IT'S NOT OVER YET.

BACK ON CHOPPER BASE--AT THE TARMAC.

STOP. WE HAVE ALL THE PROTON TORPEDOES WE NEED FOR THIS MISSION.

WELL, NOT ACCORDING TO THE WEAPONS EXPERT, WHICH IS *ME.* I WANT TWO MORE CASES OF 'EM LOADED UP.

WHY AM ***I*** THE LAST ONE TO KNOW ABOUT SUPPLY CHANGES? I ***CANNOT*** WORK UNDER THESE CONDITIONS.

UGH, IT'S LIKE AP-5 AND CHOPPER WERE MADE ON THE SAME ASSEMBLY LINE.

WHUH BUP WHUH BUP

OH, I'M THE ONE WHO NEEDS AN ATTITUDE ADJUSTMENT?

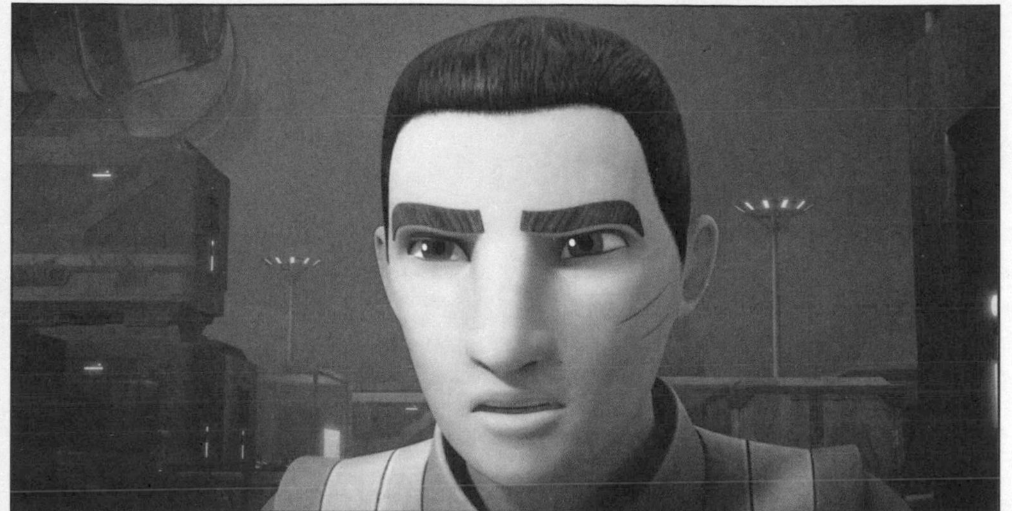

IT'S HIM. I-IT'S MAUL!

EZRA? HEY, EZRA!

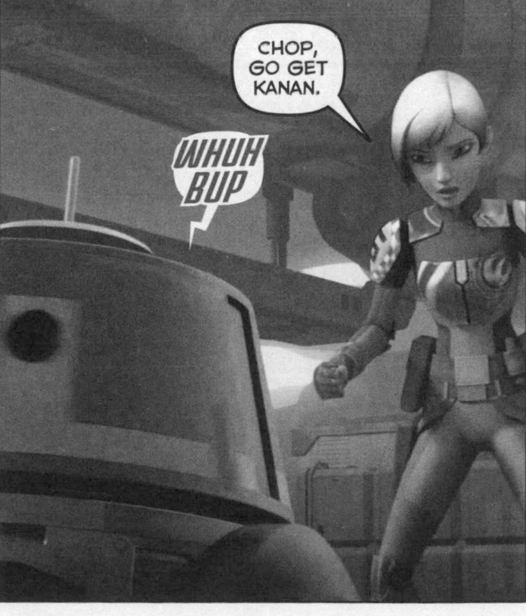
CHOP, GO GET KANAN.
WHUH BUP

OUT OF THE
WAY! THERE HE IS!
I SEE HIM.

MM-HMM-
HMM.

EZRA,
STOP!

MM-HA-HA-
HA-HA!

I KNEW IT!

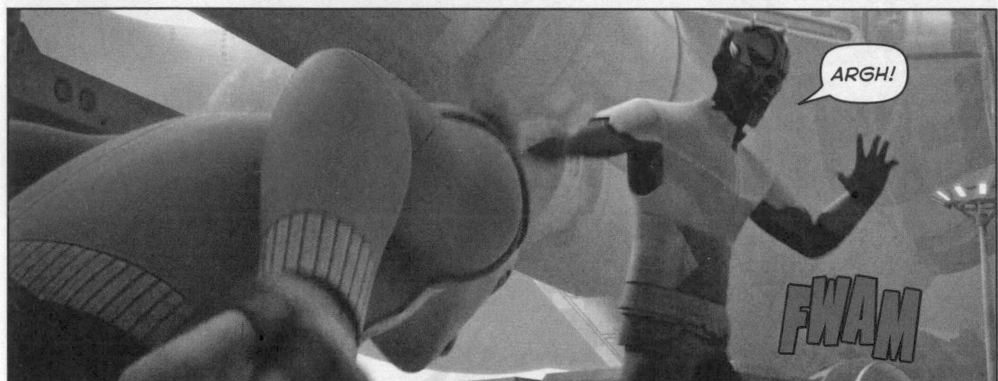
ARGH!
FWAM

FWOOSH

EZRA!

EZRA, WAIT!

LET ME GO!

TSHEWW

KANAN, WHAT ARE YOU DOING?

EZRA, IT'S NOT MAUL! LOOK AT HIM!

GASP
YOU'RE OUT OF YOUR *MIND*, KID!

I'M SORRY!

I'M SORRY!
WHAT'S *HAPPENING* TO ME?

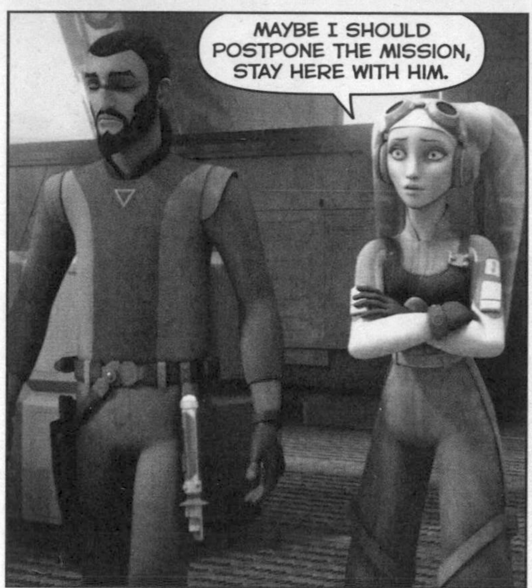
MAYBE I SHOULD POSTPONE THE MISSION, STAY HERE WITH HIM.

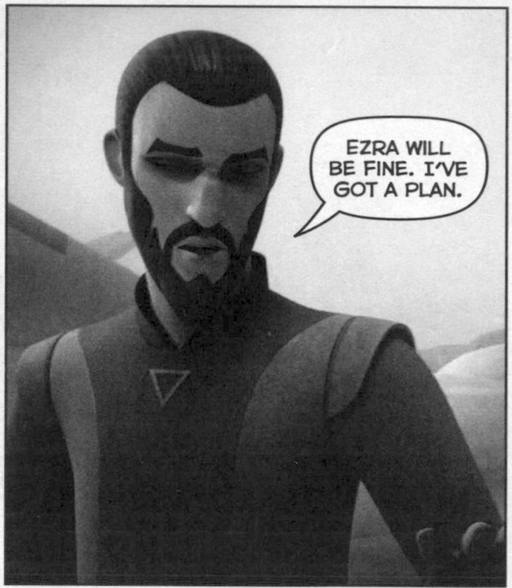
EZRA WILL BE FINE. I'VE GOT A PLAN.

SIGH
BE CAREFUL, KANAN.

WE WILL.

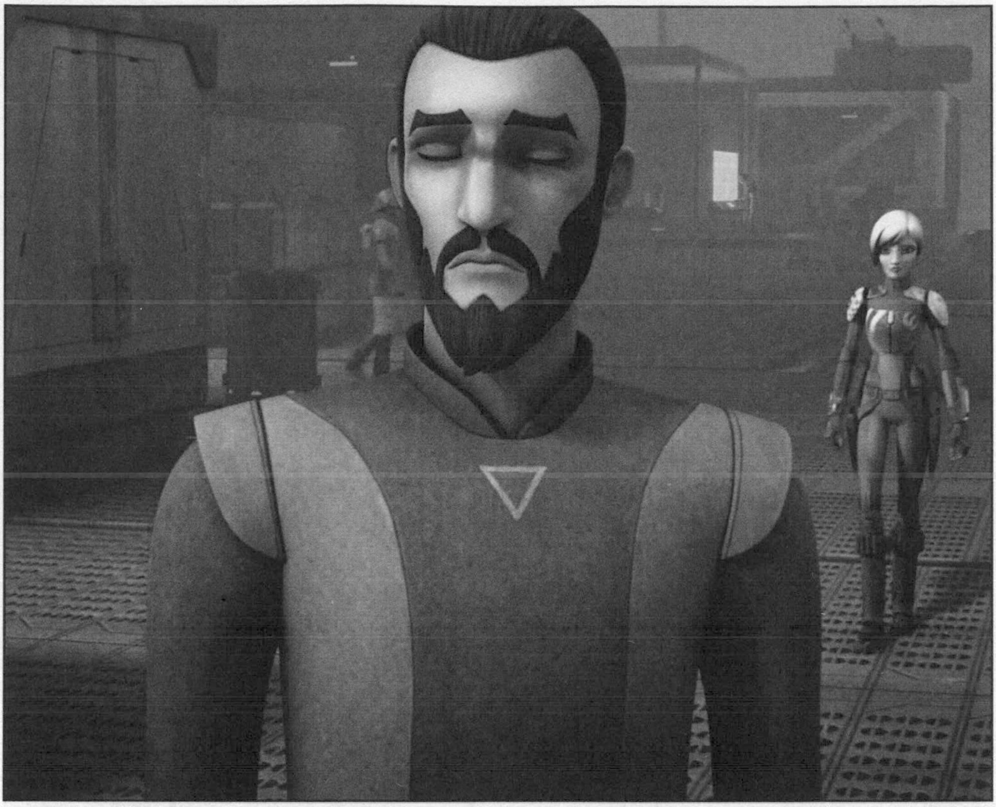

I'M SURPRISED SHE GOT ON THE SHIP.
I TOLD HER I HAD A PLAN.

REALLY? AND SHE LEFT ANYWAY?

VERY FUNNY. COME ON.

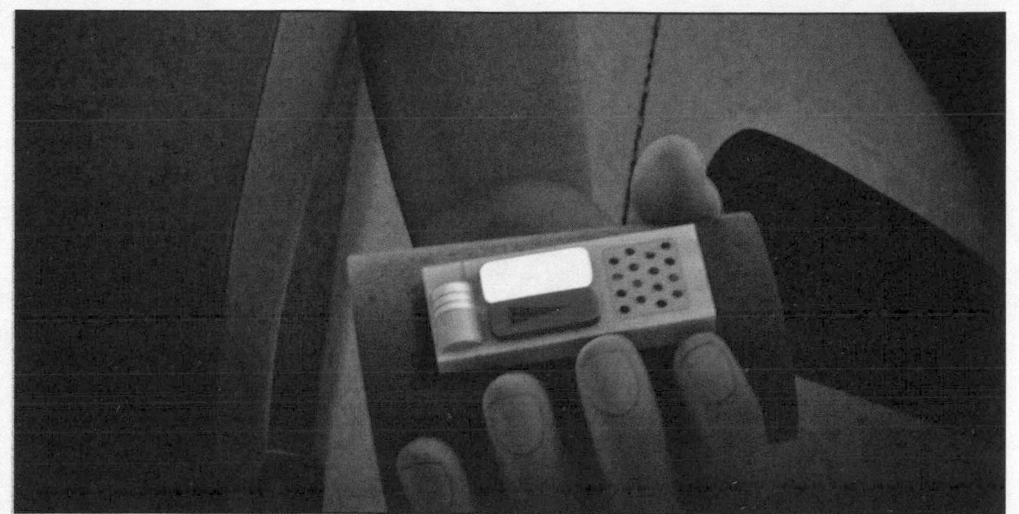

EZRA'S WRIST COMM?

I NEED YOU TO PUT A TRACKER ON IT WITHOUT HIM KNOWING.

ATOLLON--WILDERNESS.

RRRRRR

BENDU. YOU KNEW WE WERE COMING.

YES. YOU'RE NOT EXACTLY *QUIET* CREATURES, *HMM?*

TELL HIM WHAT'S HAPPENING.

THE DARK SIDE WIELDER I TOLD YOU ABOUT, THE ONE WHO WANTED TO JOIN THE HOLOCRONS TOGETHER-- I'VE SEEN HIM HERE ON ATOLLON.

I WARNED YOU--JOINING THE HOLOCRONS TOGETHER COULD BRING BOTH GREAT WISDOM AND *GREAT DANGER.*

I KNOW, I FELT THEIR POWER. AND I DID SEE THINGS, BUT MY VISION...IT WAS INCOMPLETE.

INCOMPLETE?

YEAH, I LET GO BEFORE EITHER OF US GOT THE ANSWERS WE WANTED, AND THEN THE HOLOCRONS WERE DESTROYED.

A-HA. I SEE...WELL, THAT'S NOT GOOD.

WHAT DO YOU MEAN "THAT'S NOT GOOD"? WHAT CAN WE DO?

WHAT DO YOU *WANT* TO DO, *HMM?*

I WANT TO STOP SEEING MAUL.

THEN DON'T TURN AROUND.

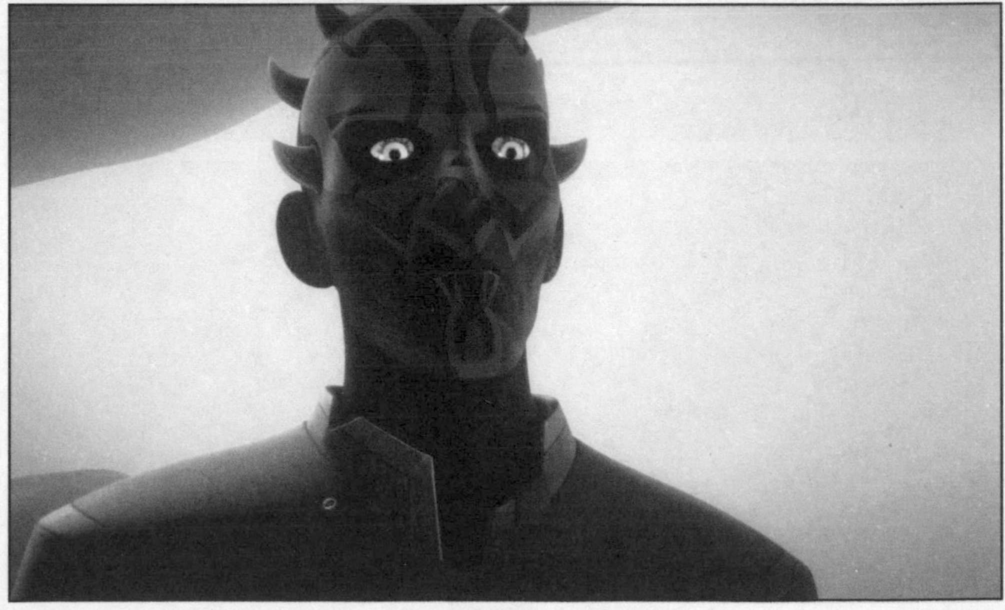

BENDU, WHAT SHOULD WE DO?
GASP

THIS IS A *STRANGE* PLACE. SO REMOTE.

OH, YES, THE EMPIRE WILL HAVE A DIFFICULT TIME FINDING YOU HERE.

TSSSHEW
TSSSHEW

YOU THINK I CAME HERE TO *FIGHT?* I CAME HERE TO SPEAK WITH MY APPRENTICE.

HE'S *NOT* YOUR APPRENTICE.
YET.

HOW DID YOU FIND ME?

WHEN YOU ABRUPTLY SEVERED OUR CONNECTION WITH THE HOLOCRON, YOU MIXED UP THE INFORMATION.
YOU LEARNED A BIT OF WHAT I WANT TO KNOW, AND I LEARNED A BIT OF WHAT *YOU* WANTED TO KNOW...

...BUT THERE WERE FRAGMENTS AND MEMORIES LEFT IN MY MIND.

LIKE THE LOCATION OF OUR BASE.

HEH. YES. VERY GOOD. OH, YOU DO LEARN FAST, APPRENTICE.

LOOK, I CAN'T MAKE SENSE OF WHAT I SAW. I COULDN'T EVEN DESCRIBE IT IF I WANTED TO.

AND *THAT* IS WHY YOU NEED TO COME WITH ME, SO I CAN RETRIEVE THE ANSWERS WHICH ARE JUST OUT OF REACH.

SO YOU GET *YOUR* ANSWERS, BUT WHAT DO *WE* GET OUT OF IT?

I WILL KEEP YOUR REBEL BASE SECRET.

NO DEAL. YOU'RE NOT WALKING OFF THIS ROCK IN ONE PIECE.

HEH-HEH. I HAVE PLANTED A BEACON NEARBY.

STRIKE ME DOWN, AND IT WILL ACTIVATE, REVEALING YOUR PRESENCE TO THE EMPIRE.

YOU HAVE KNOWLEDGE THAT IS RIGHTFULLY MINE... I HAVE KNOWLEDGE THAT YOU WANT--
--THE KEY TO *DEFEATING THE SITH.* WHAT I PROPOSE WILL SATISFY US BOTH.

ALL RIGHT.

EZRA, YOU'RE *NOT* DOING THIS.

HE'S GOING TO EXPOSE CHOPPER BASE.

WE'LL MOVE, BUILD A NEW BASE.

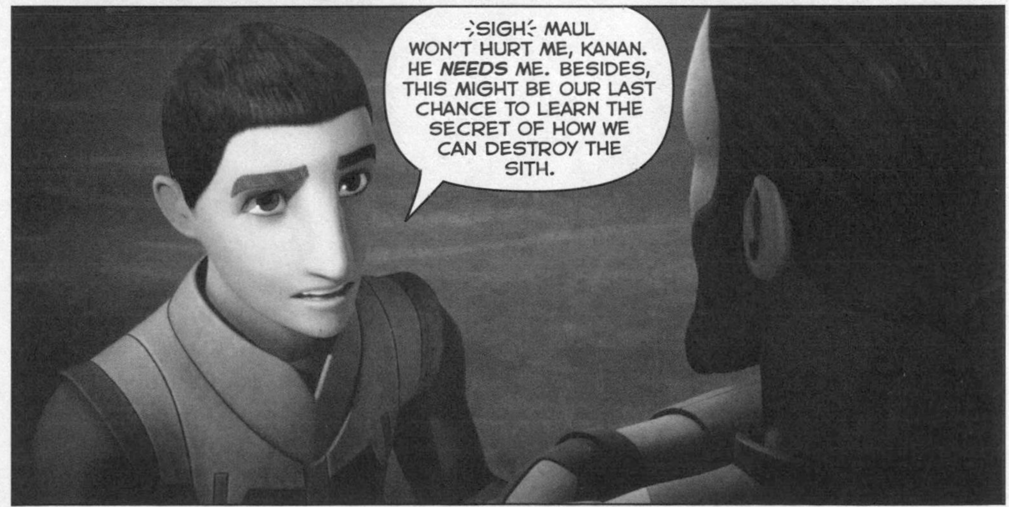
SIGH MAUL WON'T HURT ME, KANAN. HE ***NEEDS*** ME. BESIDES, THIS MIGHT BE OUR LAST CHANCE TO LEARN THE SECRET OF HOW WE CAN DESTROY THE SITH.

UGH, I DO NOT LIKE THIS, BUT WE DON'T REALLY HAVE A CHOICE, DO WE?
⁂SIGH⁂ I'M GONNA TRUST YOU ON THIS.

ALL RIGHT, WE HAVE A DEAL.

AFTER YOU, MY APPRENTICE.

I'M TRACKING EZRA'S SIGNAL. THEY JUST MADE THE JUMP TO HYPERSPACE.

LET'S GET GOING. I DON'T WANNA LOSE 'EM.

SPACE.

WHERE ARE WE?

THAT IS DATHOMIR, MY HOME.

DATHOMIR.

IF THIS IS YOUR HOME, WHERE ARE YOUR PEOPLE? WHERE *IS* EVERYBODY?

I AM THE LAST SURVIVOR. MY FAMILY, THE NIGHTSISTERS, WERE KILLED. ***MASTERFUL*** WITCHES THEY WERE--A ***THREAT*** TO THE EMPIRE. I KNOW THAT YOU CAN RELATE.

THESE WITCHES, THEY USE THE FORCE?

SOME ASPECT, YES...

...BUT IT WAS THEIR CONNECTION TO THIS PLANET THAT MADE THEM STRONG.

THAT IS WHY WE ARE HERE, TO PERFORM SOME *OLD MAGIC.*
YES. YES, EVERYTHING THAT WE NEED LIES WITHIN THE CAVE.

I'M NOT GOING ANY FARTHER UNTIL YOU TELL ME HOW THIS WORKS.

THE *ONLY* WAY TO ACCESS THE KNOWLEDGE WE SEEK IS TO MERGE OUR MINDS AGAIN. THE EFFECT WILL ONLY LAST A MOMENT, JUST ENOUGH TIME FOR EACH OF US TO FIND THE ANSWERS TO OUR QUESTIONS.

TRUST ME, EZRA, I ONLY WANT THE ANSWERS I DESERVE, NOTHING MORE.

WHAT DO WE HAVE TO DO?

COME.

DATHOMIR--TALZIN CHAMBER.

I HAVE GATHERED MANY THINGS, SECRETS TO HELP US RESTORE OUR MEMORIES.

LOOK AT ALL THIS JUNK.

DO NOT TOUCH ANYTHING.

THESE ARE ARTIFACTS FROM MY PAST, FROM A TIME WHEN MY POWER WAS ALMOST ABSOLUTE.

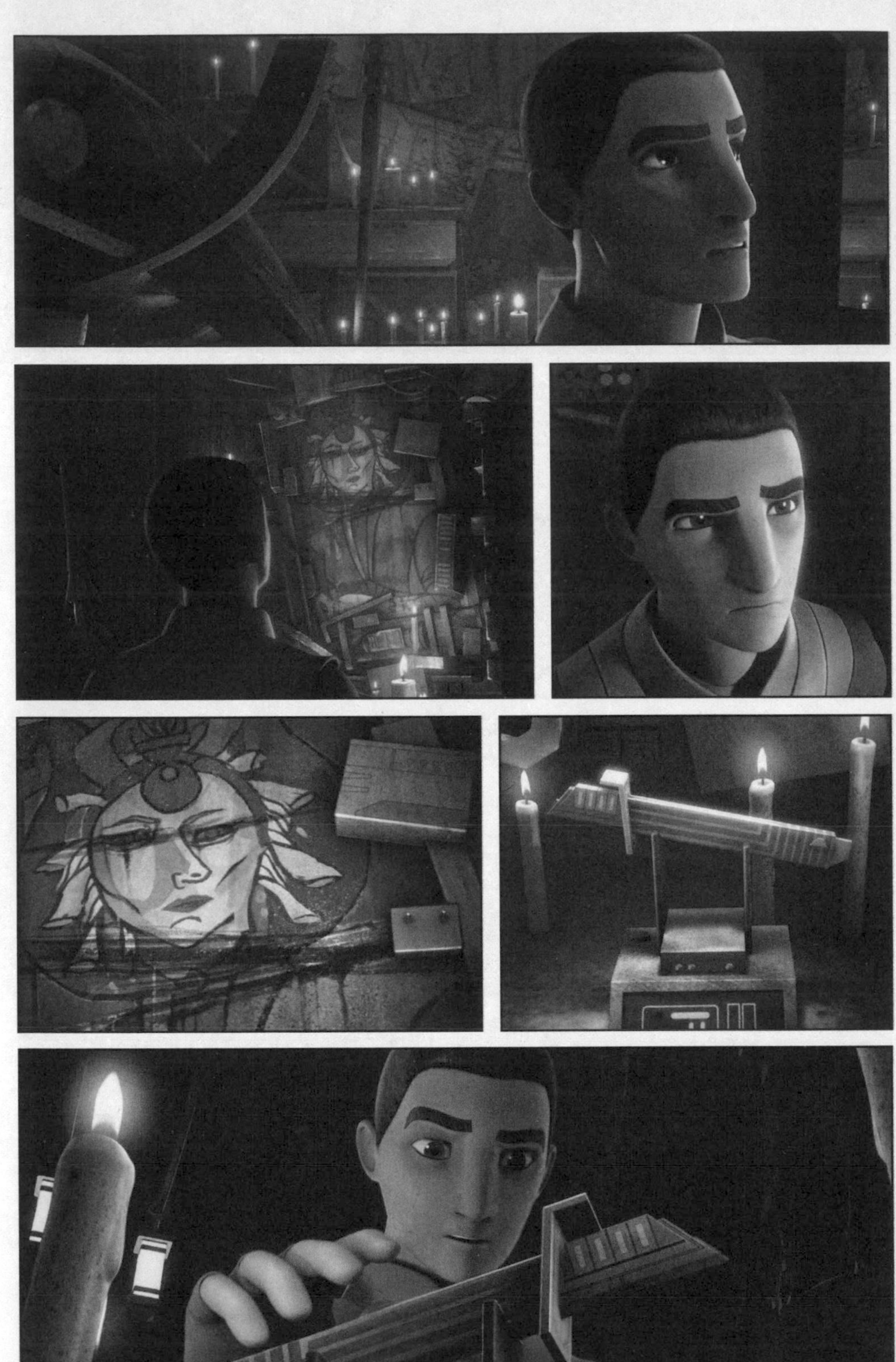

GET AWAY FROM THERE!

IS THAT A LIGHTSABER?

INDEED, YES, BUT NOT LIKE ANY THAT YOU WOULD KNOW. IF YOUR MANDALORIAN FRIEND WAS HERE...HEH...SHE COULD EXPLAIN IT TO YOU.

SPACE--OVER DATHOMIR.

WHY IS EZRA SO WILLING TO TRUST MAUL AGAIN AND AGAIN?

I DON'T THINK HE IS...BUT I DO KNOW HE'S TAKING A BIG RISK FOR ALL OF US.

DATHOMIR--ALTAR.
I HAVE STUDIED THE WAYS OF THE NIGHTSISTERS AND FOUND A SPELL THAT SUITS OUR NEEDS.

THIS... THIS ALTAR IS THE FOCUS OF THEIR ANCIENT POWER.

NOW, TO INITIATE THE MERGE, WE...

...MUST EACH DRINK THIS POTION.

MMM... YOU FIRST.

CLINK

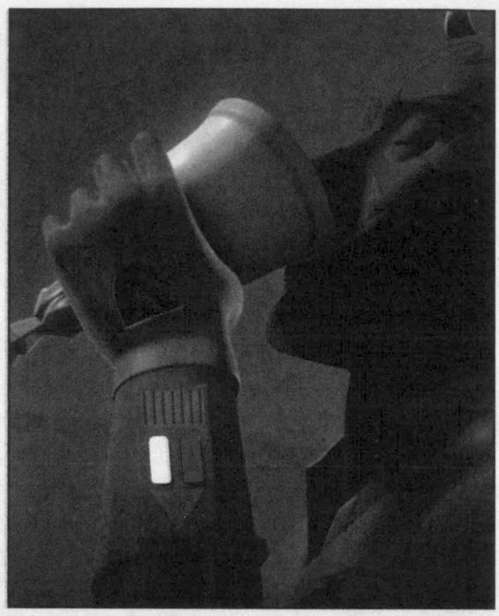

MMM. TO COMPLETE THE SPELL, YOU MUST DRINK IT ALL. JUST LIKE ME, ALL OF IT.

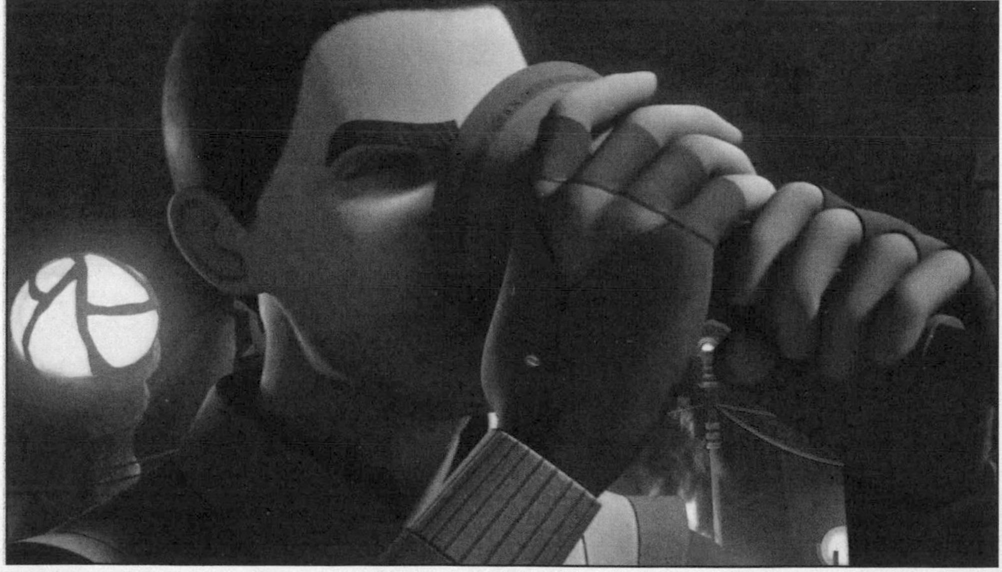

MMM, HA. IT'S... WORKING.

COUGH

SHMM
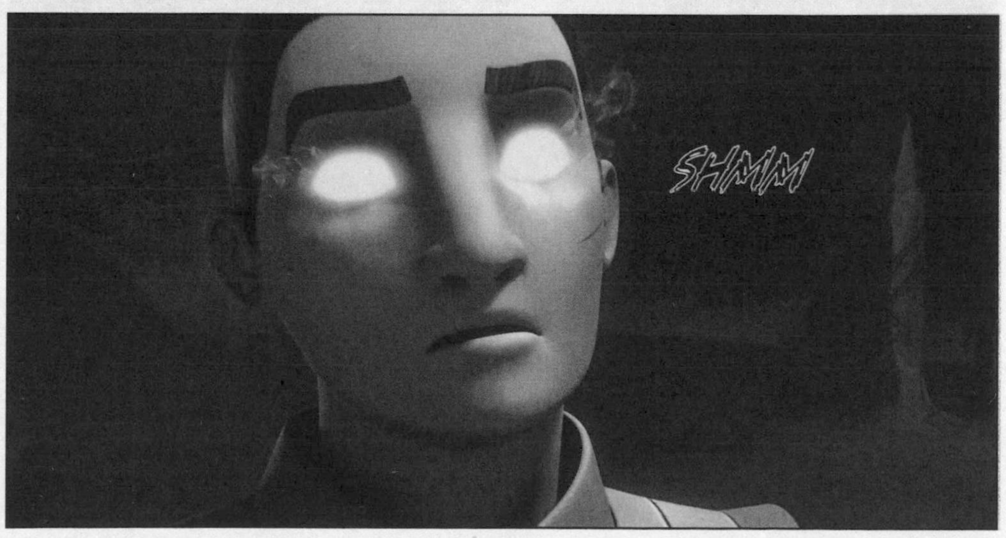
SHMM

THEY SHOULD BE THIS WAY. COME ON!

VSHHHHM

WHERE IS HE?

I WANT TO KNOW HOW TO DESTROY THE SITH.

I SEE. I UNDERSTAND.

WHO IS THAT? I-I KNOW HIM.

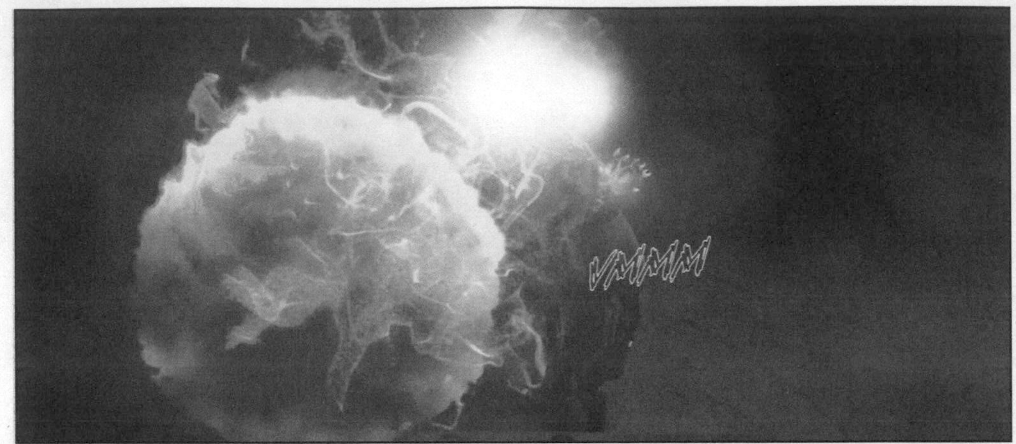
VMMM

-GASP- OF COURSE, IT ENDS WHERE IT BEGAN--A DESERT PLANET WITH *TWIN SUNS.*

HE'S *ALIVE.* I-I-I CAN'T BELIEVE HE'S ALIVE!

IT IS TIME TO PAY OUR DEBT.

WAIT, WAIT, WAIT--WHAT'S HAPPENING?

HISSSS

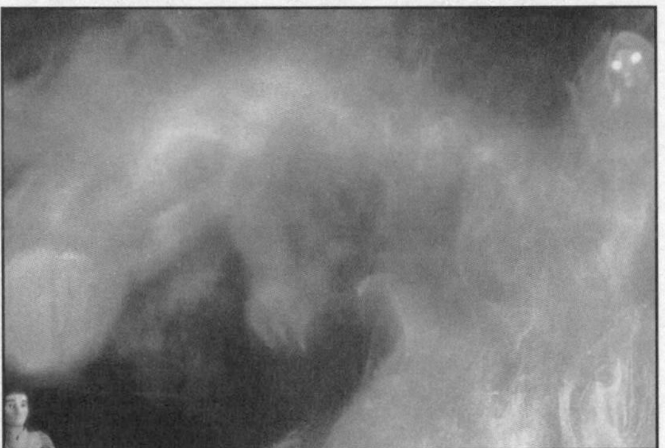

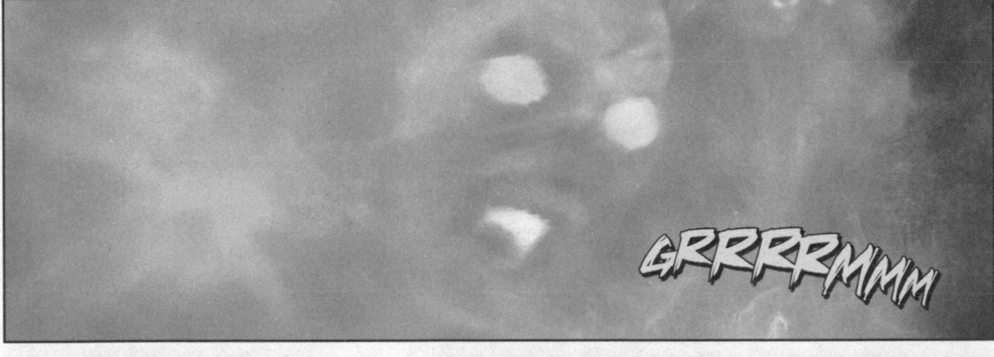
GRRRRMMM

WHAT IS THAT?

PAY OUR DUE...PAY OUR DUE...

GASP THE SPIRITS OF THE NIGHTSISTERS MUST BE COMPENSATED FOR THE USE OF THEIR MAGIC.

SO PAY 'EM, AND LET'S GET OUT OF HERE!

THE PRICE... IS OUR FLESH AND BLOOD. DON'T LET THEM TOUCH YOU!
VSSSH

NOW YOU TELL ME?

EZRA!

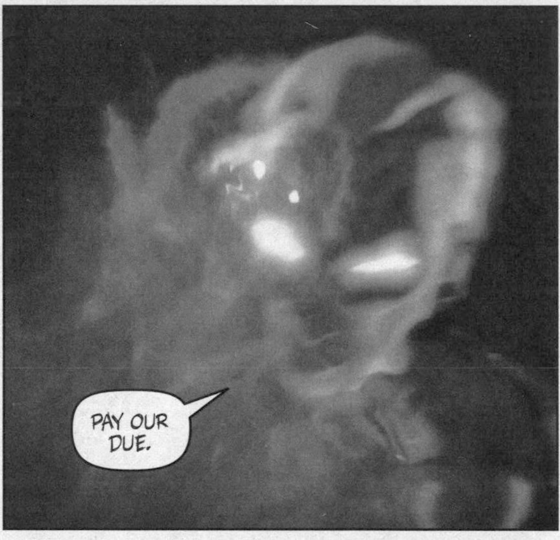
PAY OUR DUE.

KANAN, SABINE, STAY BACK!

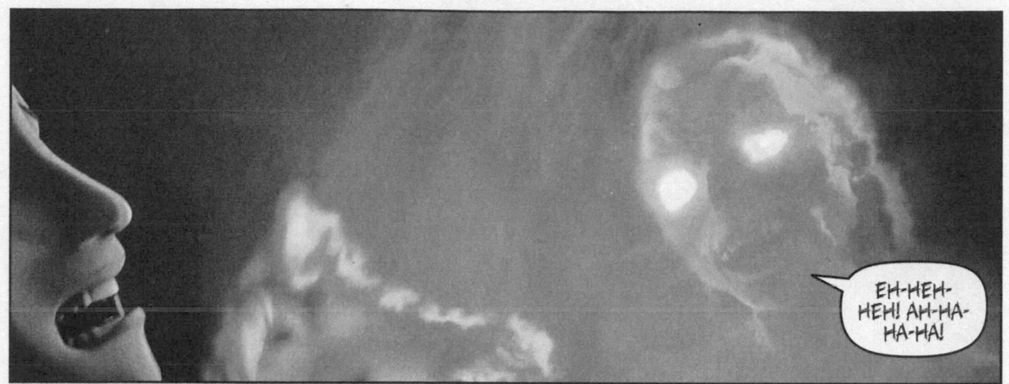
EH-HEH-
HEH! AH-HA-
HA-HA!

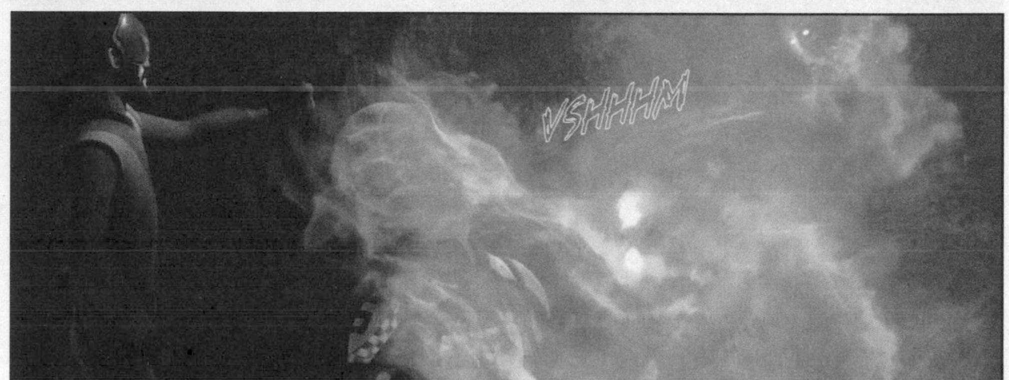
VSHHHM

AAAAAAAAAAHHHHH!
AIIIEEEEEE!

GASP

EH-
HEH-HEH-
HEH...

VMMMMM

GASP

EZRA! STAY BACK.

KANAN? SABINE?

VSSHM

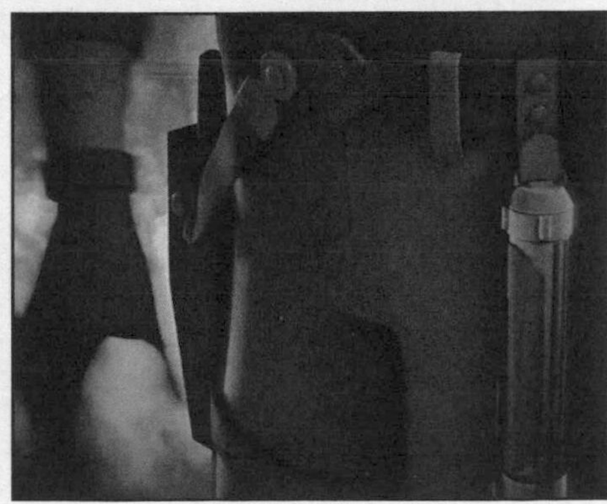

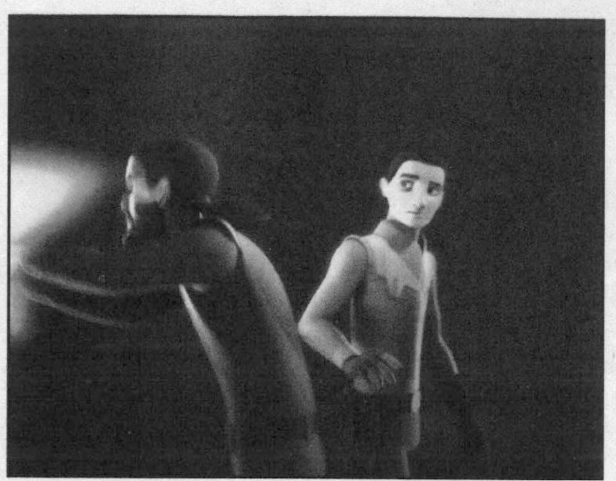

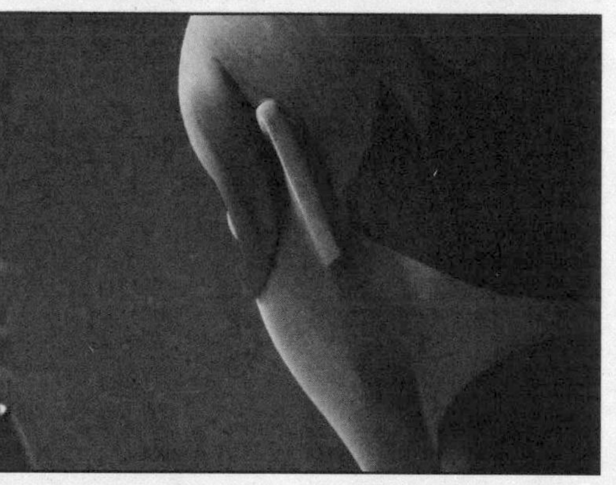

SSHM

FWAM

SABINE! IT'S EZRA!

CRKTCHAK

KTZZZZT-KRAK

YOU BETTER NOT HURT HIM!

WE *CANNOT* DEFEAT THE SPIRITS OF THE NIGHTSISTERS!

FOLLOW ME, I WILL SHOW YOU HOW TO SAVE YOUR FRIENDS.

FASTER! WE MUST REACH THE CAVE ENTRANCE.

ZRRRT

WAIT, WHY AREN'T THEY COMING AFTER US?

THE ALTAR IS THE SOURCE OF THEIR POWER. THEY CANNOT VENTURE BEYOND THE CAVE.

IT IS UNFORTUNATE ABOUT YOUR FRIENDS, EZRA, BUT THIS... THIS IS YOUR OPPORTUNITY TO EMBRACE YOUR DESTINY...

...AS MY APPRENTICE.

I TOLD YOU-- THAT IS NEVER GOING TO HAPPEN!

FORGET THE PAST! FORGET YOUR MEMORIES! FORGET YOUR ATTACHMENTS. OUR FUTURES CONVERGE ON A PLANET WITH TWO SUNS.

WE CAN WALK THAT PATH TOGETHER AS FRIENDS, AS BROTHERS.

MY FRIENDS ARE TRAPPED IN THERE BECAUSE OF US. I CAN'T JUST LEAVE THEM.

YOU DISAPPOINT ME...EZRA BRIDGER. MM-HMM-HMM.

OKAY--THE ALTAR IS WHERE THEIR POWER COMES FROM, SO, THEY CAN'T LEAVE THE CAVE...

...WHICH MEANS I JUST HAVE TO GET KANAN AND SABINE *OUTSIDE.* HOW HARD CAN THAT BE?

YOU'RE UNWISE TO REENTER OUR SANCTUM.

FWSSH

TZZK
THAT DOESN'T BELONG TO YOU.

THEN TAKE IT FROM ME, JEDI!

AAGHH! AAHHHHH!

VSHMM
NO! NO! NO! YOU CANNOT DESTROY US!
YOU'LL NEVER SAVE YOUR FRIENDS! EH-HEH-HA-HA!

VSSHHH

COUGH EZRA? WHATEVER YOU GOT OUT OF MAUL, I HOPE IT WAS WORTH IT.

DO ***NOT*** GO BACK IN THERE. THEY'LL POSSESS YOU AGAIN.

WH-WHAT ABOUT YOU? ***WON'T THEY POSSESS YOU TOO?***

I'M COUNTING ON IT!

KANAN?

VSSSS

MAUL PROMISED US FLESH AND BLOOD. WITH IT, WE CAN BEGIN AGAIN AND REBUILD THE GREAT CLAN OF THE *NIGHTSISTERS.*

IF MAUL MADE YOU THAT PROMISE, THEN IT'S *MY* DEBT AS WELL. *I* WILL PAY IT. JUST LET MY FRIEND GO.

PERHAPS, IF YOU PROVE TO BE *STRONGER.*

I KNOW *YOU'RE* IN THERE! I'M NOT LOSING *YOU* TO THESE MONSTERS!

OUR DUE MUST BE PAID!

VWMMM

FWOOSH

WHUD

SPIRIT, I AM THE ONE YOU WANT! LET HIM GO!

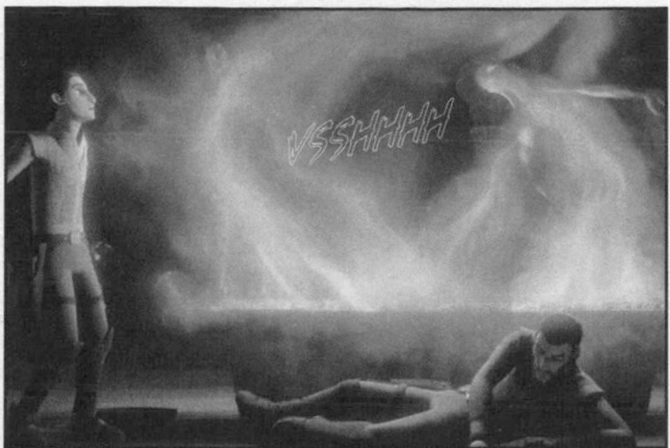
VSSHHHH

COUGH
EZRA!

YOU BELONG TO US, BOY!

KANAN, GET OUT OF HERE!

YOU BELONG TO US, BOY. THE DEBT MUST BE PAID. NOW YOU WILL PAY THE PRICE!

I'M GONNA HAVE TO OWE YOU ONE.

CRTCHAK

FTHOOM

NO! AIIIIIIEEEEEEE!

AAAAAAAAAAUGHHH!
AIIIIIEEE!

KANAN? I'M HERE.

THIS IS THE *LAST TIME* WE'RE WORKING WITH MAUL.

I SURE HOPE SO.

SABINE, I TOLD YOU TO STAY OUTSIDE.

HEY, I'VE NEVER LISTENED TO YOU *BEFORE.* WHY START NOW?

WELL, WAS IT WORTH IT? DID YOU FIND OUT WHAT YOU WANTED TO KNOW?

SIGH YES. THE ANSWER TO MY QUESTION OF HOW TO DESTROY THE SITH IS *OBI-WAN KENOBI.*

YOU THINK HE'S STILL ALIVE?

HE *MUST* BE. BUT, KANAN, MAUL'S ALSO LOOKING FOR HIM.

SO HE KNOWS WHERE HE IS NOW.

THE HOLOCRON DIDN'T TELL US THAT. IT JUST TOLD US A PLANET WITH TWO SUNS.

WELL, THAT HARDLY NARROWS IT DOWN.

WELL, WE'RE GONNA HAVE TO FIGURE IT OUT, BECAUSE IF WE DON'T FIND MASTER KENOBI BEFORE MAUL...

...THERE WON'T BE ANY WAY TO STOP THE SITH.

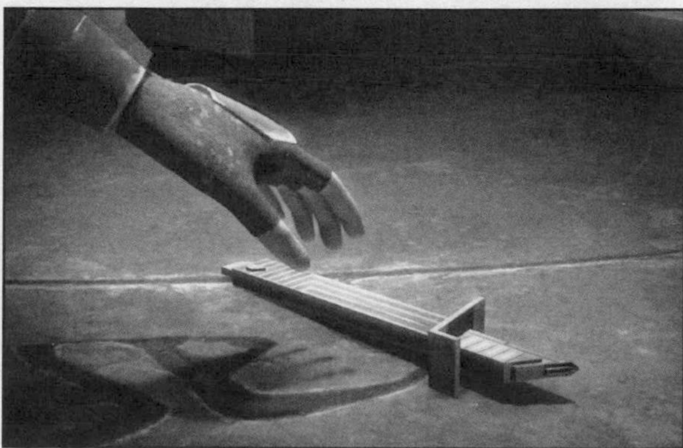

TWIN SUNS

LOST...I AM LOST.

AND YET, I CAN FEEL HIS PRESENCE...SO CLOSE... SO CLOSE...

I CAN... SEE HIM IN MY MIND'S EYE.

KENOBI...

KENOBI!

-PANT-
WILL IT END HERE? LIKE THIS?

NO. *NO!* I MUST DRAW KENOBI OUT, *TEMPT* HIS NOBLE HEART. BUT HOW? *HOW?*

I KNOW.

OOH, I KNOW.

AT CHOPPER BASE.

ZZZ...

TH-THIS IS MASTER OBI-WAN K-KENOBI. THIS IS M-MASTER OBI-WAN K-KENOBI.

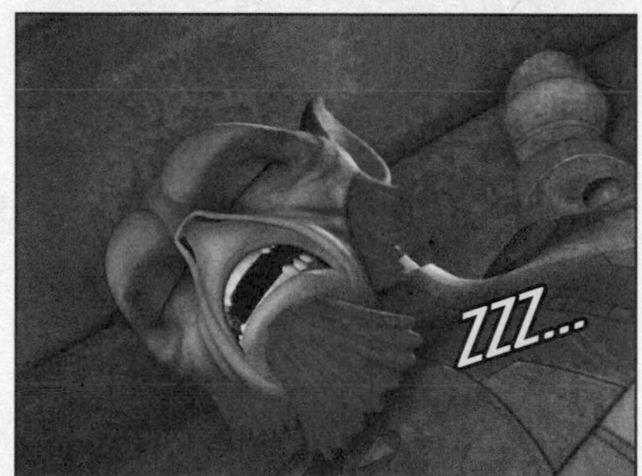
ZZZ...

THIS IS MASTER OBI-WAN KENOBI. OBI-WAN...OBI-WAN KENOBI. I REGRET...I REGRET... I REGRET...

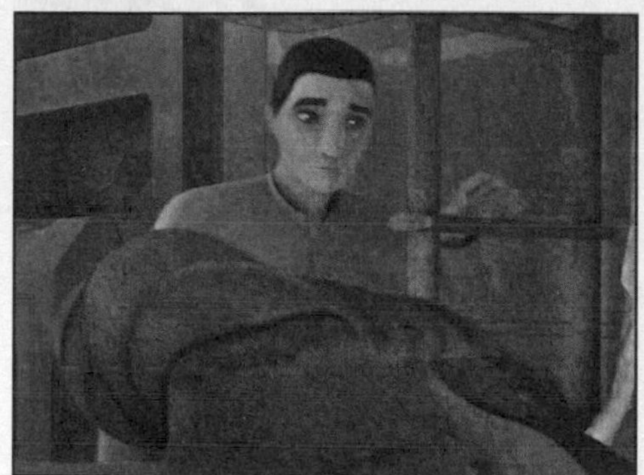

ZZZ...

THIS IS MASTER OBI-WAN...OBI-WAN KENOBI. I REGRET...I REGRET TO REPORT THAT BOTH...

...I REGRET... OUR JEDI ORDER AND THE REPUBLIC HAVE FALLEN...FALLEN...

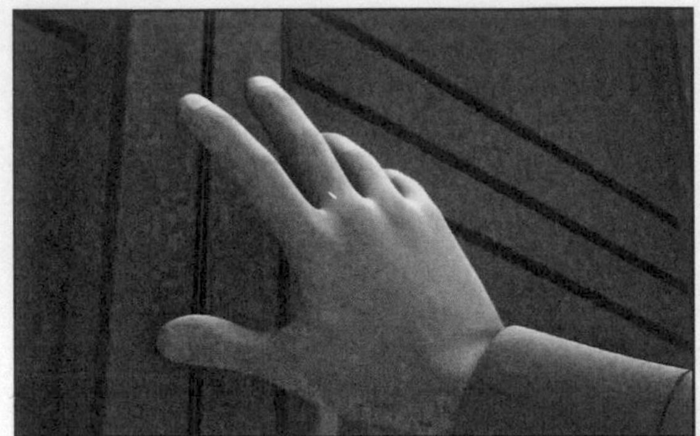

KANAN?

OUR JEDI...JEDI ORDER AND THE REPUBLIC... HAVE FALLEN WITH THE DARK SHADOW...

THIS IS MASTER OBI-WAN... OBI-WAN KENOBI.

THIS MESSAGE IS A WARNING FOR ANY SURVIVING JEDI...SURVIVING JEDI.

A NEW HOPE WILL EMERGE.

A NEW HOPE...

KENOBI.

KENOBI!

THOOM

MAUL'S
BACK.

SO WHAT DO YOU THINK
IT MEANS, KANAN?

AH, I COULDN'T
REALLY GUESS.

HOLOCRONS AT
TIMES TAKE ON A LIFE
OF THEIR OWN, BUT...AS
TO WHAT IT MEANS--

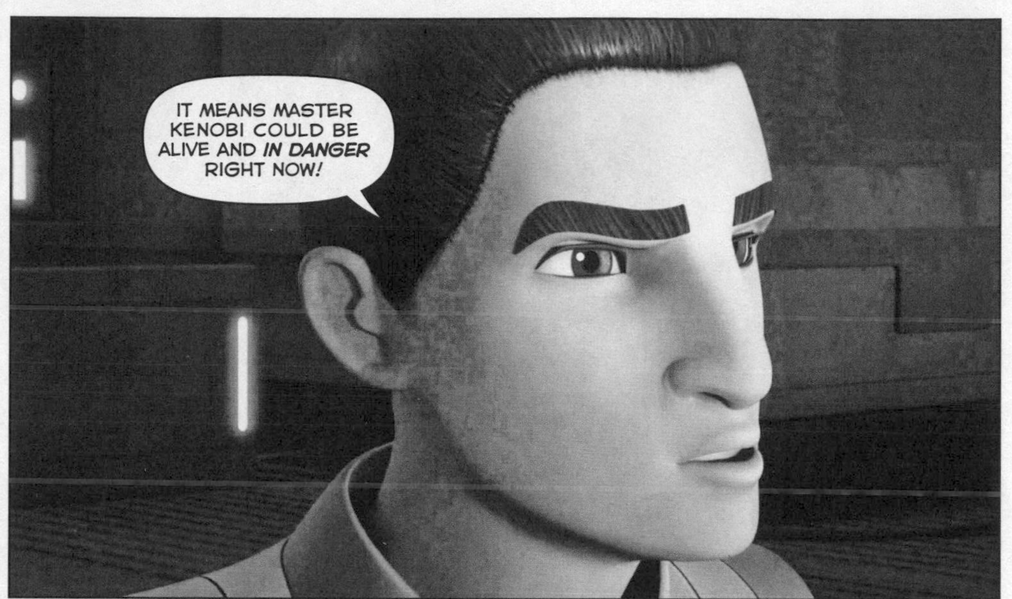
IT MEANS MASTER KENOBI COULD BE ALIVE AND *IN DANGER* RIGHT NOW!

EZRA, NO ONE WOULD LIKE TO BELIEVE GENERAL KENOBI'S ALIVE MORE THAN I WOULD...
-SIGH-... BUT SENATOR ORGANA CONFIRMED HIS DEATH.

MAYBE HE WAS WRONG. WE KNOW MAUL WENT LOOKING FOR MASTER KENOBI--THIS COULD BE A SIGN THAT HE'S CLOSING IN ON HIM!

OR IT COULD
JUST BE A BROKEN
RECORDING.

THAT DOESN'T
EXPLAIN WHY I HEARD
MAUL'S VOICE.

BUT
YOU'VE
HEARD IT
BEFORE...

YOU'VE HEARD
IT BEFORE, AND IT WAS
JUST A TRICK. MAUL WAS
MANIPULATING YOU.

I WANT TO GO TO TATOOINE TO CHECK THINGS OUT.

EZRA, CAN I HAVE A WORD WITH YOU?

WE'RE TRAINING FOR THE ATTACK ON LOTHAL, AND NOBODY KNOWS THAT PLACE BETTER THAN YOU.
I ***NEED YOU*** TO HELP US PREPARE IF WE'RE GOING TO BE SUCCESSFUL.

BUT, HERA, IF MASTER KENOBI IS ALIVE, THINK OF WHAT HE ***COULD DO*** FOR THE REBELLION.

IF HE WAS ALIVE, DO YOU THINK HE WOULD BE HIDING ON SOME BACKWATER WORLD INSTEAD OF HELPING US?

SIGH I WISH THINGS WERE DIFFERENT, I REALLY DO.

BUT RIGHT NOW, I NEED YOU HERE. THERE'S TOO MUCH AT STAKE, FOR LOTHAL...AND FOR US.

YOU KNOW I WANT TO HELP LOTHAL MORE THAN ANYONE.

I KNOW.

FWOOSH

HEY, LIEUTENANT, WHAT YOU GOT THERE?

OH, SOME MUNITIONS FOR THE A-WINGS.

WHERE DO YOU WANT 'EM?

MUNITIONS, *HUH?* WHO SENT 'EM OVER?

AP-5.

AH, AP-5. YEAH, THAT CALCULATOR'S WORKING OVERDRIVE THESE DAYS. CAN I SEE THE MANIFEST?

HEY, ANY OF THE FIGHTERS RUN FULLY LOADED?

WELL, THE TRAINER'S PREPPED. BEEN USING IT A LOT LATELY WITH THE NEWER RECRUITS.

WELL, EVERYTHING SEEMS IN ORDER, NO SURPRISE THERE.

WHY DON'T YOU TAKE THEM OVER TO...

HEY! WHAT ARE YOU DOING?

WHMMMMM

LIEUTENANT, YOU'RE NOT AUTHORIZED. *STOP!*

LIEUTENANT, COME BACK!

LAND IMMEDIATELY!

HERA, I HOPE YOU CAN FORGIVE ME.

FWSSSSSH

SPACE--OVER TATOOINE.

ALL RIGHT, HERE I AM. TATOOINE. MIDDLE OF NOWHERE.

WHUP BUH BUP BUP
AUGH!

CHOPPER!
WHUP

NO, YOU *KNOW* WHAT. HOW DID YOU GET HERE?

WHUP WHUP WHUP

I *MEAN* IN THE SHIP!

WHUH BUH
BUH BUP

I DIDN'T
WANT ANY OF YOU
TO BE INVOLVED,
NOT THIS TIME.

WHUH BUH
BUH BUHBUP

YEAH, I KNOW YOU CAN
TAKE CARE OF YOURSELF.
YOU KNOW WHAT? YOU'RE IN...
NOT THAT YOU HAVE A
CHOICE NOW.

WHUUHH BUH BUH

I DON'T KNOW WHERE WE'RE GOING...YET.

SIGH OKAY, MASTER KENOBI, IF YOU'RE DOWN THERE, SHOW ME SOMETHING.

CHOP, TAKE US IN.
I'LL LET YOU KNOW WHEN
TO CHANGE COURSE.

SHWMMMMMM

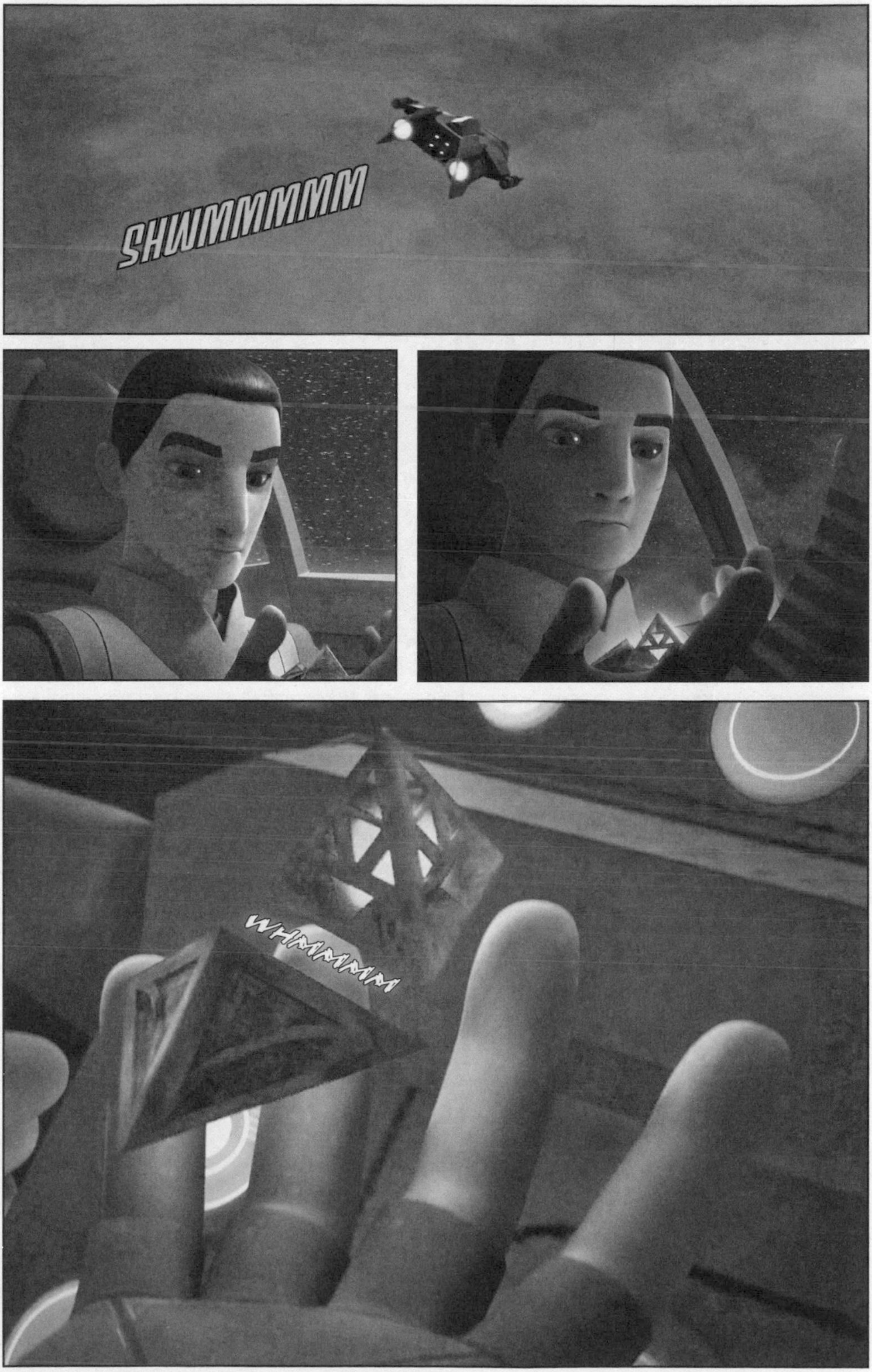

WHMMMMMM

CHOP, BRING US AROUND, NORTH BY NORTHWEST.
WHUH BUH BUP

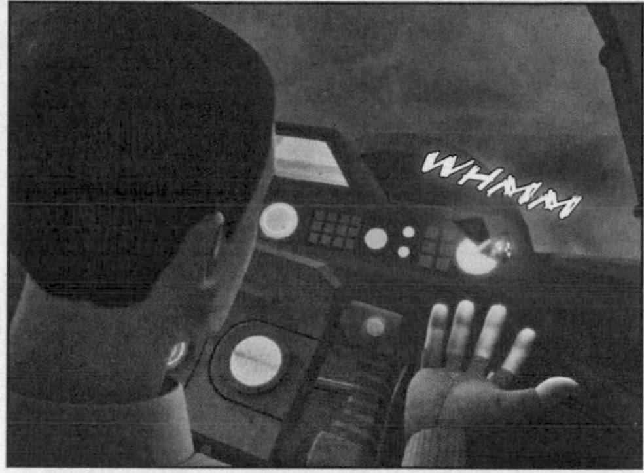
WHMM

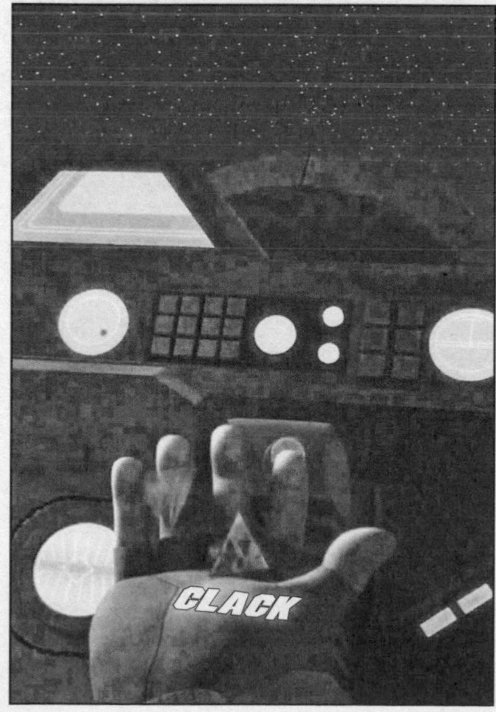
CLACK

HEY, CHOP,
TAKE US DOWN.
WAIT, WHAT?

TATOOINE--CANYON.

SHWMMM

WE'RE CLOSE NOW.

STAY WITH THE SHIP.

WHUHHH BUH BUH

WHMMM

WHMM
BUH BRRRM

SHMMMM

THE SITH HOLOCRON.
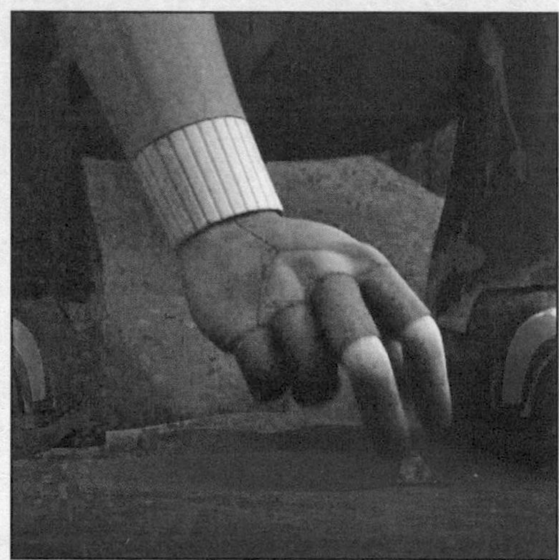

NOW...YOU... SEE...

CHOP! THIS IS A TRAP!

KRAACK

SMSSH

NNNNRRGH! YRRGH!

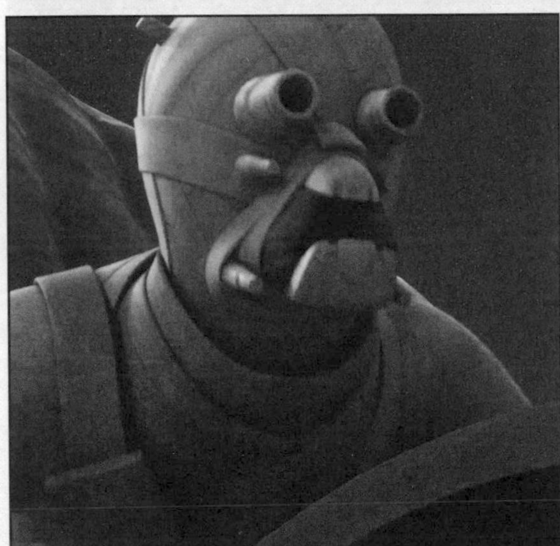

FWOOSH

FWMMMMMM

CHOPPER,
FIND COVER!

RRRRNT!
AURRRRGH!

NNNNGH!

WOOSH

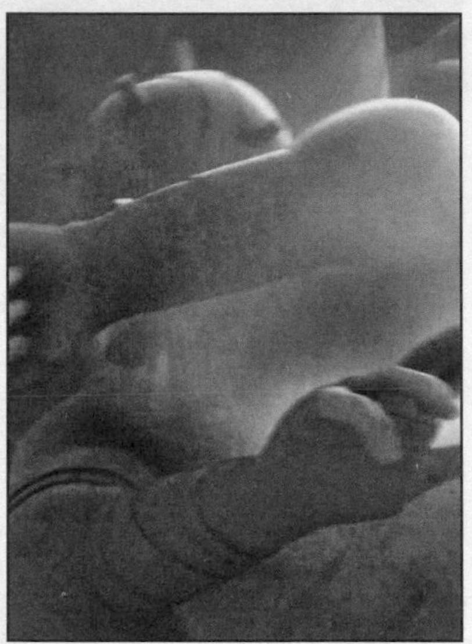

PTOOM

MOVE, MOVE!

FTOOM

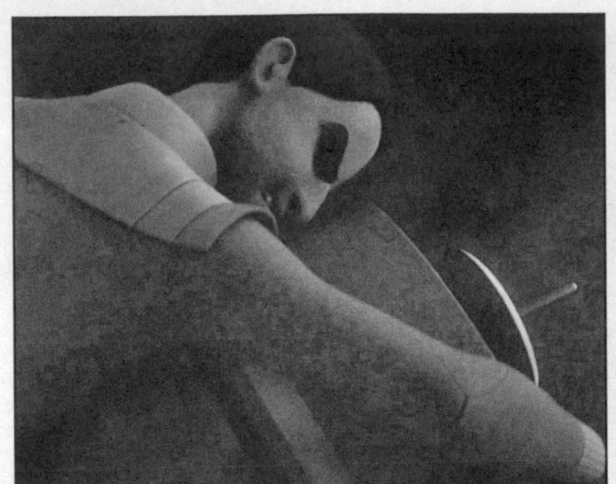

HNNNNNGH!

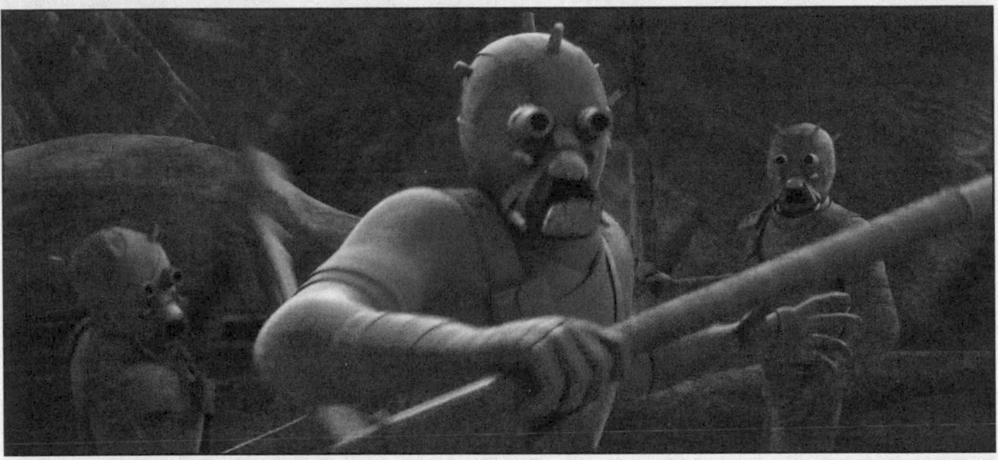

TZZZ

WELL, THAT EXPLOSION MUST HAVE SCARED THEM OFF.
WHUH BUHBUH BUHBUH BUH

WHAT ELSE *CAN* WE DO? WE HAVE TO GO FORWARD.

WHUH BUH BUH BUH

TATOOINE CANYON--MORNING.

WELL, I SUPPOSE CROSSING THE SANDS IS A BAD IDEA.
BUH BUH BUP

WUH BUHBUH BUP
YES, CHOP, ESPECIALLY FOR DROIDS.

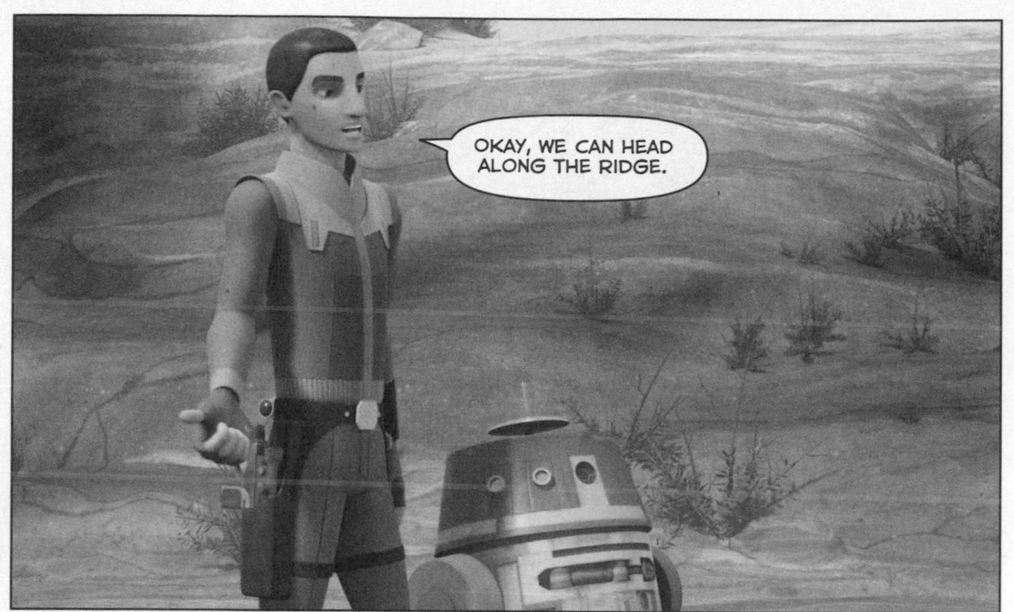
OKAY, WE CAN HEAD
ALONG THE RIDGE.

EZRA...

CHOP, YOU
SEE THAT?

WUH
BUH BUH

IT'S GONE!
IT WAS *MAUL.* IT
HAD TO BE.

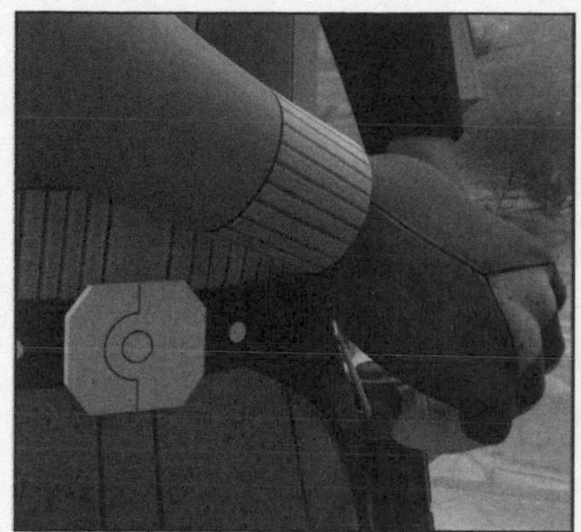

WHHHHMM

HE'S CLOSE.

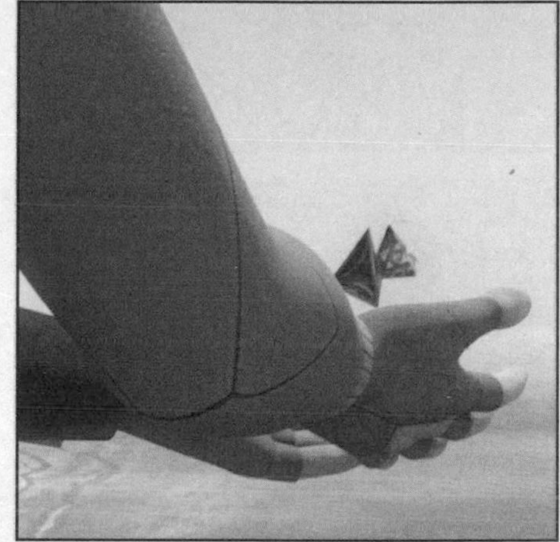

LOOK! WE HAVE TO GO THAT WAY.
WUH BUP BUP

I'M SORRY, CHOP, BUT I *HAVE* TO HELP MASTER KENOBI IF I CAN.

I'M SURE IF YOU FOLLOW THE RIDGE YOU'LL FIND A SETTLEMENT...

...MAYBE YOU COULD CONTACT HOME BASE.

WHUP
WHUHWUH WUPBUH

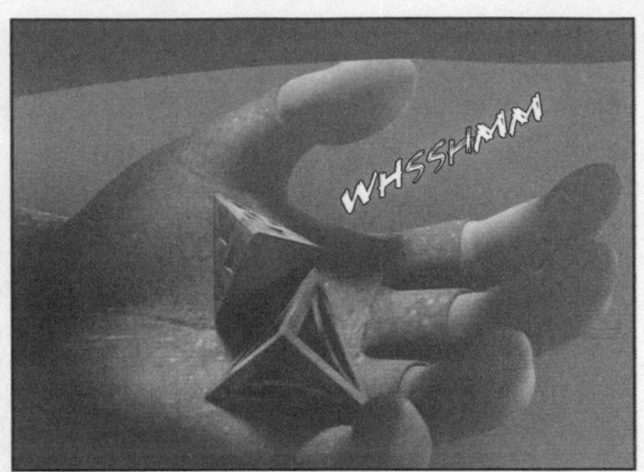

DON'T WORRY, CHOP! IT CAN'T BE MUCH FARTHER.

WE'LL FIND SOMEONE, OR-OR SOMETHING.

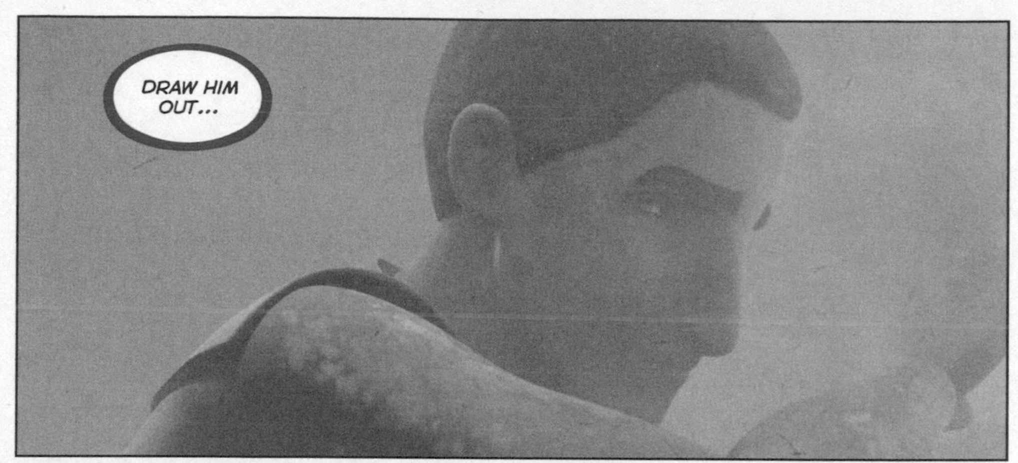
DRAW HIM
OUT...

YOUR PAIN,
YOUR SORROW...IT
CALLS TO HIM.

COME ON,
KEEP MOVING.

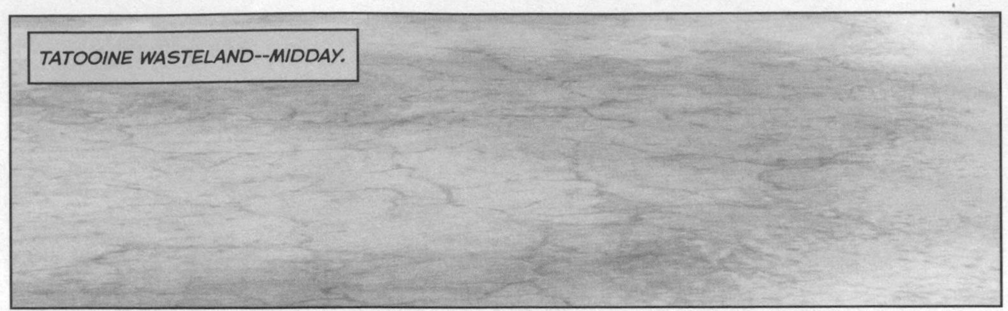
TATOOINE WASTELAND--MIDDAY.

PANT

WHUH WHUH

WHUHHMMMMMMMM

CHOP?
CHOPPER!

HEY!
NO, NO, NO,
NO, NO!

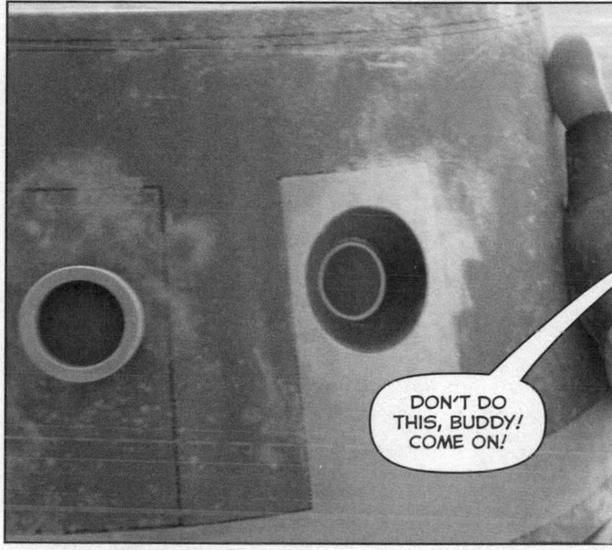
DON'T DO
THIS, BUDDY!
COME ON!

CHOPPER!
HEY, CHOPPER!

:SIGH:
THIS IS MY
FAULT.

I SHOULD HAVE JUST
STAYED HOME.

I DON'T KNOW
WHAT TO DO.

HE IS DEAD...
HE IS DEAD.
NO.

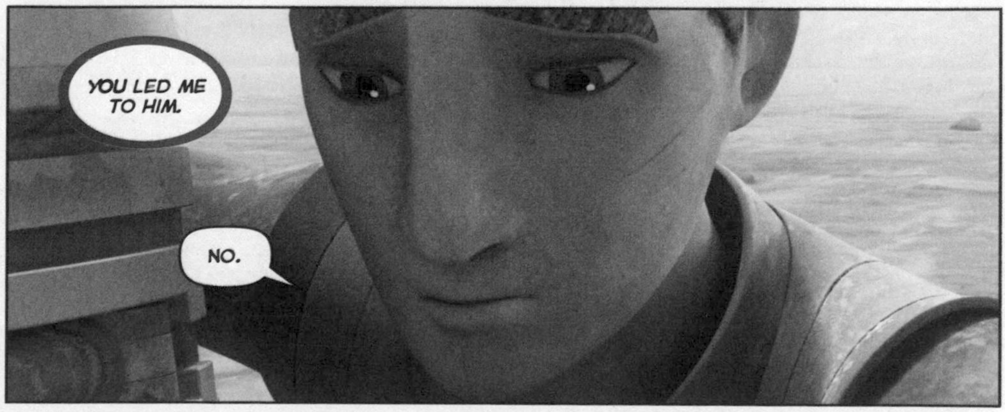
YOU LED ME
TO HIM.
NO.

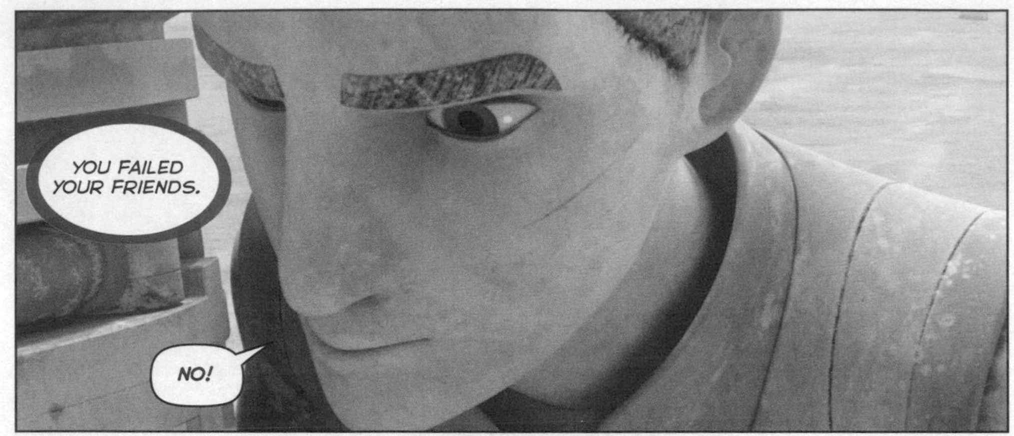
YOU FAILED YOUR FRIENDS.
NO!

YOU WILL DIE!

NO!

UGH.
WHUD

MM-HMM-HA-HA-
HA-HA-HA...

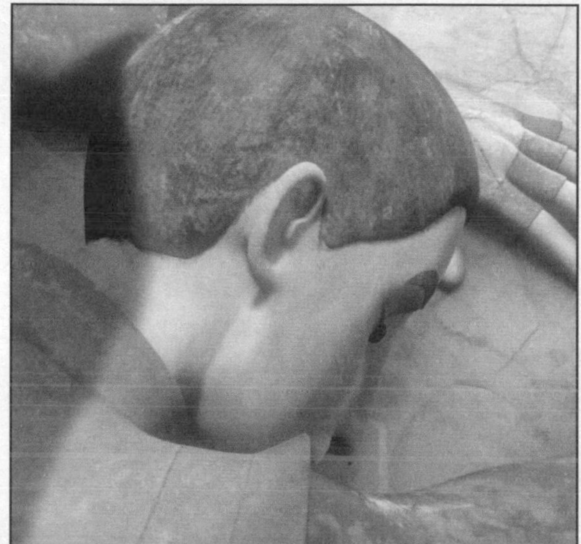

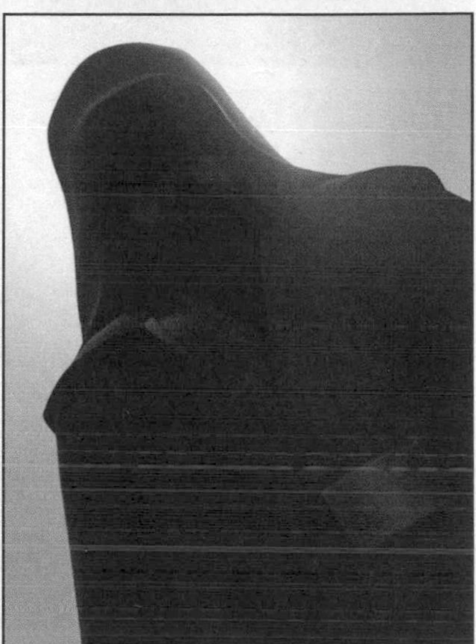

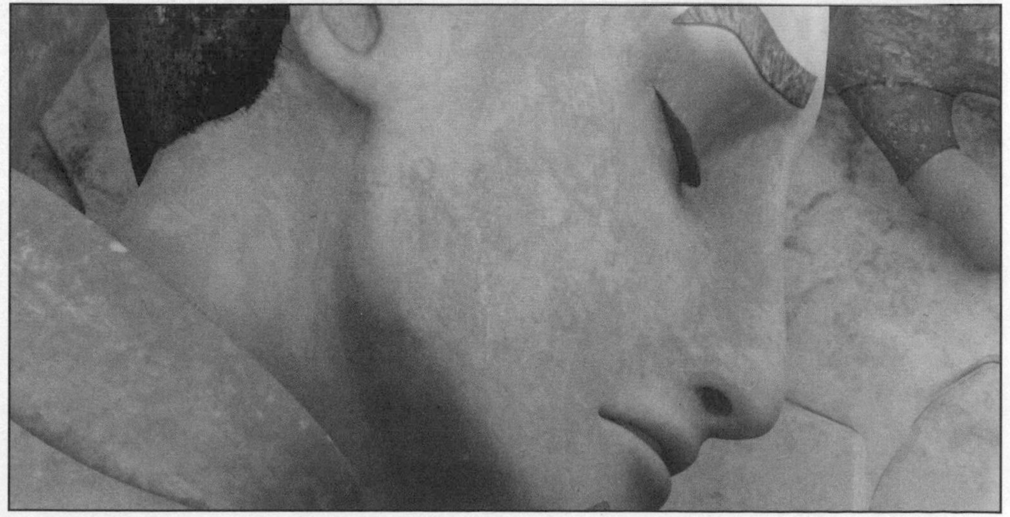

TATOOINE WASTELAND--NIGHT.
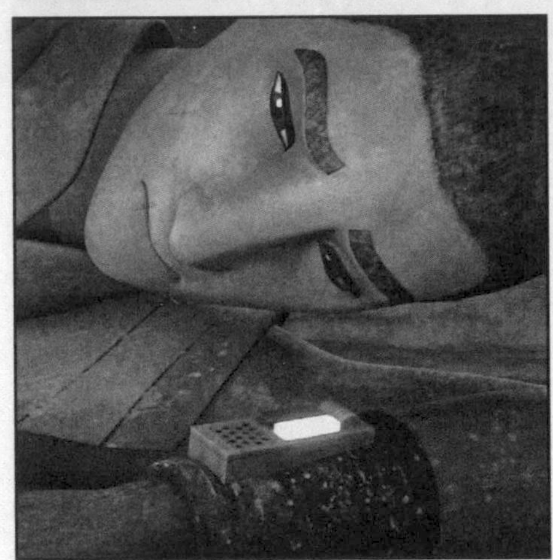

RRRGHH

WHUH BUH
BUP BUP

YOU'RE IN THE WRONG PLACE, EZRA BRIDGER.

MASTER? *MASTER KENOBI!?*

I AM. AND WHEN YOU HAVE YOUR STRENGTH, I WILL HELP YOU ON YOUR WAY.

ON MY WAY? NO, I CAME HERE TO FIND YOU! TO *WARN YOU.*

ABOUT MAUL?

YES! YOU KNOW?

ONE DOESN'T SURVIVE AS LONG AS I HAVE BY BEING FOOLISH OR UNPREPARED.
MAUL IS AN OLD ADVERSARY, AND A *PERSISTENT* ONE AT THAT.

WE CAN FIGHT HIM TOGETHER!
I HAD NO INTENTION OF FIGHTING HIM, THOUGH THAT SEEMS INEVITABLE NOW.

YOU DON'T UNDERSTAND-- *YOU'RE* THE ANSWER. THE HOLOCRONS TOLD ME!
THEY SAID YOU WOULD BE THE ONE TO HELP US DESTROY THE SITH.

HMM. IT'S THE FIRST I'VE HEARD OF IT.

THE REBELLION NEEDS YOU. WE NEED YOU TO DEFEAT THE EMPIRE.

WHAT YOU NEED, YOU ALREADY HAVE.

UNFORTUNATELY, YOU SEEM TO BE LETTING IT ALL GO.

BUT IF I HAD WHAT I NEEDED, WHY WOULD THE HOLOCRONS SEND ME TO YOU?

THEY DIDN'T. *MAUL DID.*

MAUL USED
YOUR DESIRE TO DO
GOOD TO DECEIVE YOU,
AND IN DOING SO, HE
HAS ALTERED THE
COURSE OF MANY
THINGS.

HE KNOWS YOUR
FEARS, YOUR HEART,
AND HE MANIPULATED
THE TRUTH...

...WHICH HAS LED
YOU HERE, WHERE
YOU SHOULD *NEVER*
HAVE BEEN.

BUT THE HOLOCRONS,
THEY TELL THE TRUTH.

DO THEY? THE TRUTH IS OFTEN WHAT WE MAKE OF IT. YOU HEARD WHAT YOU WANTED TO HEAR...
...BELIEVED WHAT YOU *WANTED* TO BELIEVE.

AND NOW, THE ONLY ONE WHO HAS GAINED ANYTHING FROM ALL OF THIS IS...

ME.

YOU MUST GO NOW.

I LED HIM TO YOU. LET ME MAKE IT RIGHT.

THAT IS NOT YOUR RESPONSIBILITY. I WILL MEND THIS OLD WOUND.

RIDE NORTH. THAT IS YOUR WAY OUT...

...YOUR WAY *HOME.*

NRRAH

SEE YOU SOON, APPRENTICE.

SIGH LOOK WHAT HAS BECOME OF YOU. A *RAT* IN THE DESERT.

LOOK WHAT I HAVE RISEN ABOVE.

I'VE COME TO KILL YOU, BUT PERHAPS IT'S WORSE TO LEAVE YOU *HERE,* FESTERING IN YOUR SQUALOR.

WHY COME TO THIS PLACE? NOT SIMPLY TO HIDE.

OH, YOU HAVE A *PURPOSE* HERE. PERHAPS YOU ARE PROTECTING SOMETHING?

NO...PROTECTING SOMEONE.

TSSSHEW

TSSSHEW

TKZZZ
HRRAAAGH!
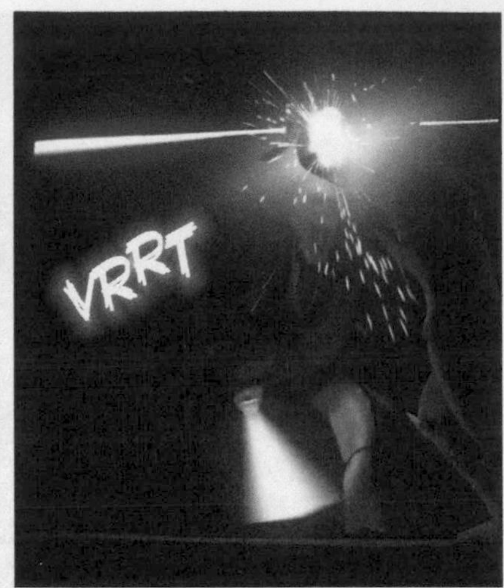
VRRT

TELL ME. IS IT THE CHOSEN ONE?

HE IS.

HE...WILL... AVENGE US.

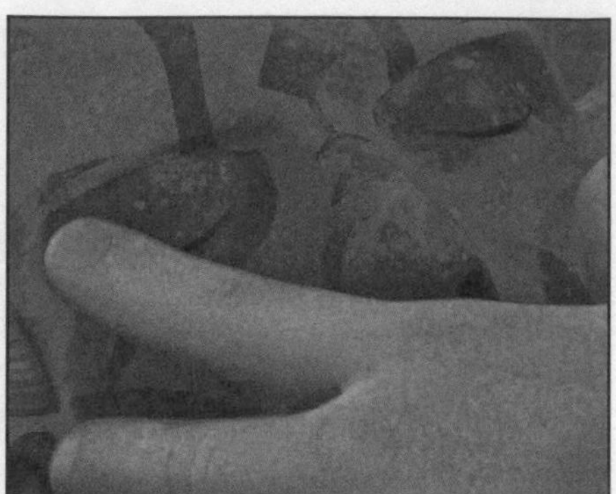

CHOPPER BASE, ATOLLON.
FWWMMMM

TELL ME THIS MEANS WHAT I WANT IT TO MEAN.

WE WON'T BE SEEING MAUL AGAIN.

WELL?

I'M SORRY I RAN OFF LIKE THAT-- I WAS WRONG.

THIS IS WHERE I'M SUPPOSED TO BE. YOU'RE MY FAMILY...

...AND WE SHOULD GO HOME.

TATOOINE DESERT.

LUKE? LUKE!

TO BE CONTINUED...

CREDITS

Created by: Simon Kinberg, Dave Filoni, and Carrie Beck
Based on Star Wars created by George Lucas

"Twilight of the Apprentice: Part 1"
Executive Producers: Simon Kinberg and Dave Filoni
Coexecutive Producer: Henry Gilroy
Supervising Director: Dave Filoni
Director: Dave Filoni
Producer: Kiri Hart
Writers: Simon Kinberg and Steven Melching

"Twilight of the Apprentice: Part 2"
Executive Producers: Simon Kinberg and Dave Filoni
Coexecutive Producer: Henry Gilroy
Supervising Director: Dave Filoni
Director: Dave Filoni
Producer: Kiri Hart
Writers: Dave Filoni and Simon Kinberg

"The Holocrons of Fate"
Executive Producers: Simon Kinberg and Dave Filoni
Coexecutive Producer: Henry Gilroy
Supervising Director: Justin Ridge
Director: Steward Lee
Producers: Kiri Hart, Carrie Beck, and Athena Yvette Portillo
Writer: Henry Gilroy

"VIsions and Voices"
Executive Producers: Simon Kinberg and Dave Filoni
Coexecutive Producer: Henry Gilroy
Supervising Director: Justin Ridge
Director: Bosco Ng
Producers: Kiri Hart, Carrie Beck, and Athena Yvette Portillo
Writer: Brent Friedman

"Twin Suns"
Executive Producers: Simon Kinberg and Dave Filoni
Coexecutive Producer: Henry Gilroy
Supervising Director: Justin Ridge
Director: Dave Filoni
Producers: Kiri Hart, Carrie Beck, and Athena Yvette Portillo
Writers: Dave Filoni and Henry Gilroy